What the sidewalk shoppers are saying about Jennifer and Charles—that couple in the window:

"Why is the window so steamy tonight? I can't see what they're doing!"
—Henrietta, age 82

"That mousy 'bride' is hardly Charles Derring's type. It should be me living in the window with him!"
—Delphine, Charles's soon-to-be ex-girlfriend

"Jennifer never wore pink silk teddies for me! This is an outrage."
—Peter, Jennifer's soon-to-be ex-boyfriend

"Derring Brothers Department Store's sales are up 20%!"
—Jasper Derring, owner and Charles's father

"How much is that couple in the window?"
—Timmy, age nine

Dear Reader,

"What should I give my sweetheart for Valentine's Day?" women ask as February 14 draws near. Bestselling author Marie Ferrarella offers a one-of-a-kind gift idea: *The 7 lb., 2 oz. Valentine*—which is also book three of her wonderful cross-line series, THE BABY OF THE MONTH CLUB.

In *The 7 lb., 2 oz. Valentine,* Erin Collins is a mom-to-be, but the unknowing dad-to-be hasn't been seen in months. And when he does turn up, he doesn't remember *anything*—let alone her! Next month, look for book four of THE BABY OF THE MONTH CLUB series in Silhouette Desire.

Lori Herter, one of *Yours Truly*'s launch authors, presents her own valentine to you—*How Much Is that Couple in the Window?*—book one of her irresistible new miniseries, MILLION-DOLLAR MARRIAGES. Jennifer Westgate has to live in a department store's display window with a make-believe husband—for an entire week of newly wedded bliss! Look for book two of this fun series in August.

Next month, you'll find two *Yours Truly* titles by JoAnn Ross and Martha Schroeder—two new novels about unexpectedly meeting, dating…and marrying Mr. Right!

Happy Valentine's Day!

Melissa Senate

Editor

Please address questions and book requests to:
Silhouette Reader Service
U.S.: 3010 Walden Ave., P.O. Box 1325, Buffalo, NY 14269
Canadian: P.O. Box 609, Fort Erie, Ont. L2A 5X3

LORI HERTER

How Much Is that Couple in the Window?

Published by Silhouette Books

America's Publisher of Contemporary Romance

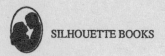 SILHOUETTE BOOKS

ISBN 0-373-52014-X

HOW MUCH IS THAT COUPLE IN THE WINDOW?

Copyright © 1996 by Lori Herter

About the Author

LORI HERTER was an only child and learned to entertain herself by daydreaming. Now happily married, she has found a good use for her well-developed imagination by writing romance novels. She's written mainstream vampire romances, a novel for Silhouette Shadows—*The Willow File* (SS#28)—and contributed a novella to the 1993 Silhouette Shadows anthology. These days, Lori has turned her attention to writing romantic comedy.

Her first Yours Truly novel, *Listen Up, Lover* (8/95), was one of the line's two launch titles. *How Much Is that Couple in the Window?* is book one of her new miniseries for Yours Truly, MILLION-DOLLAR MARRIAGES. "Hope you enjoy it!" Lori says from California, where she lives with her husband, Jerry, and their three cats.

**To Pat Teal, my longtime agent and friend—
thanks for a great idea!**

1

After his usual early breakfast of coffee, dry wheat toast and marmalade, Jasper Derring walked into the windowed sun-room of his Chicago lakefront mansion. His wife of forty years, Beatrice, brought him the morning paper. He opened it and on page five found what he wanted to see—a full-page Christmas ad for Derring Brothers Department Store.

The huge ad dazzled with artistic flair. Large snowflakes danced against a black background. Darting between the white flakes, Santa and his reindeer all but jumped off the page. Santa's sack on the sleigh was huge and on it was printed:

Derring Brothers' gift to you: No toy trains. No artificial snow. No dancing elves or talking bears. Nor will Rudolph with his light-bulb nose clutter our store windows this year. Only Derring Brothers is daring enough to present fully live, breathing *people* for you to gaze at in a living tableau—*real* persons celebrating the holiday season just the way you do at home. People you've seen at work in our store, who have served you with the capable courtesy Derring Brothers is famous for. Come by our North Michigan Avenue windows during the week before Christmas and see for yourself. Wave hello! *Our* merry display people can see you and wave back!

Jasper was pleased with the ad his son, Charles, had commissioned. The living window display had been Charles's idea. Jasper had thought it outlandish at first, but quickly saw possibilities in the promotional event that even Charles hadn't imagined—and still had no notion of.

Charles had taken over Derring Brothers when an unexpected heart attack had forced Jasper into partial retirement six months ago. Used to being in charge all his life, Jasper found it difficult to let go and give control of the department store that he had founded with his brother over forty years ago to his younger son. But of all his grown, scattered, errant children, Charles was the most dependable. He had a natural aptitude for business, not to mention a highly creative mind. And, unlike his siblings, Charles had always loved the department store, ever since he was a towheaded, runny-nosed kid.

Jasper set aside the newspaper. The morning was too beautiful, with sunshine on the snow outside the windows and a cardinal by the bird feeder, to spend it reading about political scandals and crime reports or even the Dow Jones averages. Instead, he picked up his needlepoint project.

He'd taken up needlepoint, a lifelong hobby of his wife's, when he was recuperating from his heart attack. His wife had suggested it because he'd been so fidgety and out of sorts being stuck at home. She'd told him that it always calmed her and focused her. Beatrice had shown him how to do the two basic stitches, the continental and the basket weave, and he'd begun on a small Christmas stocking. Once he'd gotten into it, he'd become hooked, much to his wife's surprise. He'd started making gifts such as glasses cases and decorative pillows for family members, as Beatrice had often done over the years. Jasper tended to go overboard in the local needlepoint shop and bought everything that caught his eye. He currently had enough hand-painted canvases to stitch to keep him busy for the next three years.

Strangely, he found himself buying several canvases that commemorated wedding days, even though he didn't know of anyone in the family getting married. He realized it had been an unconscious wish to see his children, all of whom were still stubbornly single and happy that way, married before he died. His doctor had given him a good prognosis, and Jasper seemed to have made a remarkable recovery, but the heart attack had made him realize he wouldn't be around forever to oversee his huge, amassed fortune or to guide his children—not that they particularly wanted any guidance.

He picked up the canvas he'd been working on, an intricate design of flowers and stems twined with wedding bells. It was finished except for an empty space in the middle section, which Jasper hadn't begun yet. There the names of the newly married couple were to be stitched, along with their wedding date. He ought to put the project aside for now and wait for someone to announce they were getting married. That's what his wife often did with her projects; then she had them ready for shower gifts when a baby was born or a wedding was announced.

Instead, Jasper decided to think positively. Perhaps focusing on the project would make what he wanted to happen happen faster. He'd learned to do that in business and knew that halfhearted plans and goals never unfolded the way they ought to. So, Jasper decided to finish the project—or at least stitch in the names. He could leave the date for later. He threaded his needle with burgundy French cotton perle and began work on a capital *C,* the first letter of the first name of the prospective groom. Won't Charles be surprised! Jasper thought with a mischievous little chuckle. He would be even more surprised if he saw the name of the bride Jasper was planning to stitch in beside Charles's name.

Yawning, Jennifer Westgate opened up the morning edition of the *Chicago Tribune* she'd bought at the Elmhurst commuter train station. All at once, her sleepy eyes widened as a familiar name in huge print at the top of the page caught her by surprise.

DERRING BROTHERS DEPARTMENT STORE

She read the text on the Santa Claus sack and her mouth dropped open. So the rumors were true!

Jennifer rolled her eyes uneasily toward the train window she sat next to. Picturesque suburban houses with snow on their roofs sped by, but her mind was on the full-page ad. For weeks now, she'd heard coffee-break gossip about the new publicity idea. She couldn't believe they would really put store employees on display in the windows. If they wanted real people instead of mannequins, why didn't they hire professional models?

As a Derring Brothers employee, Jennifer might be chosen. The thought made her feel slightly ill. She wasn't a shy person, but she wasn't an exhibitionist, either. And if she was chosen, what would Peter think? She kept telling herself she shouldn't worry about it. The store had hundreds of employees. Why would they pick her?

Still, she had an odd feeling that she'd wind up involved. Just last week, Mr. James, a makeup expert she'd often seen doing make-overs in the cosmetics department, had mysteriously shown up in Housewares, where she worked. For some reason, he'd made a beeline for her and struck up a disjointed conversation about automatic drip coffeemakers. All the while, he seemed to be studying her, apparently analyzing her features and skin. Soon he shifted the conversation and suggested that some mauve eye shadow would bring out the color of her green eyes. She'd told him straight out that she didn't like wearing makeup. She felt makeup was a facade and she wanted people to accept her as she was, not artificially enhanced. Mr. James looked perplexed, then amused, and walked off with a Cheshire-cat smile.

But that wasn't the only incident that had made her suspicious. About a month before that, Jasper Derring himself had also made a silent study of her. It had happened on a Wednesday, on one of Jasper's infrequent visits to the department store since his heart attack. The short, eccentric, sixtyish millionaire, wearing his customary tweed hat with a feather on one side, was walking through Housewares—why, she didn't know. He stopped when he saw Jennifer and seemed to single her out, his brown black eyes sparkling from beneath his bushy gray eyebrows. He stared at her for a long moment with a peculiar focused energy in his gaze. She'd smiled hesitantly in response, not knowing what he was thinking or what his purpose was. He'd nodded to her, absently commented that it was a nice day—even though it was snowing outside—and rather mysteriously gone on his way.

What such special notice from the store's grand old man meant, Jennifer had had no idea. In the past, he'd occasionally stopped to talk to her briefly, and other than feeling honored, she'd never thought anything of those encounters. But this time, she'd gotten the feeling that he had secrets to keep. Later she heard rumors about a living holiday window display using store employees, and she began to wonder.

But then again, maybe she was just being paranoid. She hoped so. Having her head examined by a psychiatrist sounded far more appealing to her than standing in a window all day and having every person who walked down North Michigan Avenue turn and stare at her.

Jennifer was twenty-six and had worked as a saleswoman for Derring Brothers for five years. Recently, she'd been proud to be promoted to assistant manager of Housewares. She loved the store and liked most of the people working there. Jasper Derring had a well-deserved reputation for instilling comradery and loyalty in his employees, and he returned their loyalty with a fair salary, good benefits and opportunity for promotion. If she was going to stay in retail sales, she wouldn't work anywhere else.

However, things had changed in the past several months. Jasper Derring, though still part owner of the store, was no longer its president. After his heart attack last July, he'd turned the store over to his son, Charles Derring, who immediately became the new president. He'd also given Charles half ownership.

Since that turn of events, Derring Brothers had taken on a different atmosphere. The store's former stately quality was disappearing. Everything from the antique glass showcases to the gold-painted molding on the ceiling was being "updated," the word used in advisory memos from the new president to the employees. The store was quickly losing its familiar classic style and taking on a slick modern veneer. Along with this, the TV and newspaper ad campaigns had become "high profile"—*gaudy* was the word Jennifer would have used—rather than the quality ads they used to have. She supposed the window display idea was also a part of the store's new image, and that this new image was all Charles's doing.

Jasper might be eccentric, but he had both feet on the ground. He also had class, the type of class that comes not from money, but from character. Jasper was a man who had been married to the same woman for decades, who raised hothouse orchids on his Kenilworth estate and had some of his flowers made into corsages or boutonnieres for his employees when their birthdays came. He believed in old-fashioned values like courtesy, integrity and giving the customer good value for his or her dollar. He believed in hard work, because he had come up the hard way himself, going from selling yard goods with his brother off the back of a truck to owning his own multimillion-dollar retail corporation. Expensive clothes, flashy cars, fancy parties and playboy ways were never his style.

His son, Charles, however, was a whole other story.

"I'll bet you any money it was Charles's idea," Jennifer said to Trudy Hargrove later that morning. She'd arrived at work early as usual. "He has that screwball side to him. Like when he programmed my register with those crazy messages."

She was referring to her birthday earlier in the year when her new computer cash register suddenly flashed "Happy Birthday, Jennifer!" at her while she was ringing up a sale. The following week, it flashed "I've got an itch at the back of my terminal—can you scratch it for me?" She didn't know how to get rid of the message and had to wait until it mysteriously disappeared before she could continue using the register. She knew Charles had done it, because he was the only one in the department at that time who had access to the cash registers and the computer knowledge to program them.

"It's just like him to come up with a publicity stunt like this," she told Trudy.

"I don't doubt it," Trudy agreed as she studied the newspaper ad. A competent woman in her late forties with a smart haircut that made her prematurely gray hair enviable, Trudy was the manager of the Housewares department and Jennifer's boss. "Charles was an incorrigible cutup when he worked with us. Being president doesn't seem to have changed him, as far as I can tell."

At the beginning of the year, Charles had served as the temporary manager of Housewares for four months. Their original manager had quit and Charles had taken his place until Trudy was made manager. Charles had been filling in when vacancies turned up in the store's various departments for the past three years. He'd readily told everyone with his characteristic enthusiasm—and perhaps to impress his father—that it was his intention to learn every facet of the department-store business from the ground up, clearly anticipating that he would one day take over the store.

That day had arrived sooner than most employees had expected, due to Jasper's sudden heart attack. Charles was only thirty-one when he became president, and many of the older employees quietly remarked to one another that he hadn't "settled" yet. Was Jasper wise, permanently turning the store over to his rambunctious son so soon?

"So," Trudy said, lifting a carefully penciled eyebrow as she glanced at Jennifer, "the question is, which employees will be chosen for the window?"

"Heard any new rumors about that?" Jennifer asked. "I keep having that awful feeling it'll be me." She had told Trudy about Jasper Derring and then Mr. James studying her for no discernible reason.

"I did hear from Grace in Cosmetics that they've hired Mr. James to show up every morning the week before Christmas."

"Well," Jennifer said with false hope, "that ought to rule me out—I told him I hate makeup."

Trudy smiled. "If we could all look so good without it! You'd be as lovely as you always are in a window under the lights."

"Thanks, but it hasn't exactly been my aim in life to be a mannequin on display for everyone to gawk at." Jennifer took her name badge out of her handbag and pinned it to the lapel of her navy wool suit jacket. "The newspaper ad even encourages people to come and wave at the models in the window. I can't imagine anything more embarrassing. It would be like living in a cage at the zoo! And it's such a weird idea. How could Jasper Derring approve of this stunt?"

"It *is* quite a publicity stunt, all right," Trudy agreed. "A bit of Charles's derring-do." It was a joke among the employees, often repeated.

"A piece of Derring doo-doo, if you ask me," Jennifer said.

"Shh!" Trudy whispered with a throaty chuckle. "You know better than to say that out loud around here!"

"Derring doo-doo, Derring doo-doo," Jennifer repeated defiantly.

"Memo for Jennifer Westgate."

She found herself interrupted by a young man named Rick, who had been hired as a messenger for the executive offices. He was smiling at what he'd caught her saying.

"For me?" she said, too wary of the envelope in his hand to be embarrassed. She had that feeling again of being on the threshold of something awful.

"You got the wrong name tag on today?" Rick asked.

"No."

"Then this is for you, from the prez himself." He handed it to her and walked off.

Trudy came to her side. "From Charles? Well, open it! What's it say?"

"I hope it says I'm fired," Jennifer told her with gallows humor as she tore the envelope open. She skimmed the brief, typewritten memo.

Dear Jennifer,
You have been selected to be the female model for our holiday window display the week before Christmas. That week only, your work hours will be from 10:00 a.m. to 10:00 p.m. A generous bonus will follow. I think we should have lunch today and discuss it.
                              Best, Charles Derring

"Oh, God, it's happened." Thunderstruck and slightly sick to her stomach, Jennifer turned the memo over to Trudy.

"For heaven's sake! You *have* been chosen," Trudy said with excitement. "Don't look so distressed. It'll be fun! And you'll get a bonus, too!"

"I wonder if he did this on purpose," Jennifer said, not caring about the bonus.

"Who? Charles?"

"I'll bet he picked me to get back at me. He always blamed me that day he split the seat of his pants, remember? When I accidentally on purpose spilled the glass pebbles on the floor?" When they'd worked together early in the year, she'd spilled the slippery pebbles used in flower vases near his cash register, to pay him back for programming the surprise messages on her register. When he was squatting to pick them up, the back center seam of his pants had split. "He wants to humiliate me in return. Well, I won't do it!"

"Jenny," Trudy said in a motherly tone, "calm down. They've probably done a lot of marketing research for this window display idea. You weren't chosen for some petty reason, I'm quite certain. Take it as a compliment. And it wouldn't be smart to refuse to do it. You don't want to be marked as uncooperative, not willing to give your all, if you intend to get more promotions in the future."

Jennifer chewed her fingernail and glanced at her watch. It was one minute till opening time. Soon, holiday shoppers would be pouring in. "I suppose you're right," Jennifer conceded. "But you know how Charles always liked to needle me."

"He still does, whenever he passes by." There was a hint of amazement in Trudy's voice. "And you needle him right back—with gusto, I've noticed. You two bicker so much, a casual observer might think you were married."

"No way! He prefers glittery blondes anyway." A new thought came to her. "Who else will be in the window display besides me? Are they picking male employees, too? Will there be teams, maybe alternating two hours on and two off?"

"Connie in PR said she heard they were choosing only one woman and one man."

Jennifer was appalled. "What! I'm going to be the *only* woman on display for seven days? How can they expect anyone to stay in a window for twelve hours straight? What am I supposed to be doing all that time—a juggling act? And who's going to be the man?"

Trudy shrugged. "Don't know. It was only a rumor. Maybe Connie had it wrong."

"I can just imagine what Peter will think of all this," Jennifer fretted.

"Peter? You're going to be famous for a week, get a nice bonus, and you're worrying about your absentminded professor? It might light a fire under him. How long have you been dating him?"

"Three months."

"And he's barely kissed you."

Jennifer wished she hadn't lamented about her love life to Trudy so much. "He's an English professor. Academic people conduct their lives with a certain reserve."

"Disdain is more like it," Trudy murmured under her breath.

"I just know he'll take a dim view of his girlfriend appearing in a store window. It'll be an embarrassment for him." Jennifer slammed her fists on the glass countertop in exasperation, shaking the bun warmers on display. "Oooh!" she exclaimed. "Why me? Why did they pick me? I'm not glamorous or anything. I'm not what you'd call sexy, not with my plain old brown hair and flat chest. Why would they stick me in a store window?"

"Peter?" Jennifer said when a male voice answered the University of Illinois number she'd dialed. Peter taught at the Chicago campus on the west side of the city.

"Jennifer?"

"Yes, it's me. Sorry to bother you. I'm on coffee break, so I won't talk long. I just wondered if you would have dinner with me tonight. I've got something I need to talk over with you."

"Mmm." Peter seemed to be checking his calendar. "It happens I'm free. All right. Shall I pick you up at six? Or are you working late tonight?"

"No, but I may be . . . soon."

"Are you all right? You sound upset."

"I am, a little. I'm . . . afraid you will be, too."

"Really?" he said, a touch of concern in his deep, authoritative voice. "I can arrange to meet you for lunch, if that will help."

"Thanks, but I can't. I'm having lunch with the president."

"Charles Derring?"

"Yes. I was summoned by a memo this morning. Look, I can't talk now. See you at six, okay?"

Jennifer hung up after he said goodbye and walked away from the pay phone. She was in the third-floor employees' lounge. Sighing, she got a cup of coffee and headed toward a table where others on break were sitting. Her co-workers were talking about their children and grandchildren, always a favorite topic.

Jennifer barely heard them. All she could think about was that Peter would disapprove of what she was being asked to do. Peter didn't even think she should be working in a department store. She had two years of college to her credit, and Peter was always telling her she ought to go back and get her degree and then get a "meaningful" job. She often argued with him, saying there was a great deal of potential for her at Derring Brothers, but he never seemed impressed.

Now that she was being asked to be a mannequin in the window, Peter would have new ammunition. How could she argue?

She could think of only one hope. Maybe at lunch she could talk it over with Charles and ask him to choose someone else. To a small degree, they *were* friends, despite the practical jokes they'd played on each other during the four months they'd worked together. And even though he thought she was straitlaced and razzed her about taking life too seriously, she felt that he did like her.

Charles might be wild and wacky—and rich and powerful, too, she reminded herself—but he had a heart. Sometimes. It was worth a try anyway.

2

Just before noon, Jennifer looked up from the shelf she was kneeling in front of, rearranging glassware, and found Charles Derring standing a few feet away, watching her.

"Hard at work as ever," he said with dry amusement. His blond hair was combed back neatly and he wore an expensive pin-striped suit. His silk tie was colorful, artistic and tasteful, and looked hand-painted. Charles had a natural, if unintentional, flair for looking like he'd been named to Mr. Blackwell's best-dressed list. She'd never observed him preening himself; he always looked effortlessly smashing. He had a square-jawed, handsome face to match his wardrobe and sunny blue eyes. He was so perfect-looking it didn't seem fair that he should be a millionaire in the making, too. Not to mention that he was also the youngest downtown Chicago department-store head that anyone had ever heard of.

"Just trying to impress the prez," she said in response to his hard-at-work comment. Then she chided herself that she ought to show more respect. After all, he *was* the president, and she shouldn't call him prez to his face.

Charles cleared his throat importantly. He lowered his voice with authority. "Yes, I do like to see my employees hard at work." His expression changed and his tone grew more wisecracking. "In your case, however, I'd like to see you slack off once in a while, just to prove you're human."

"Am I going to get another all-work-and-no-play lecture?" Jennifer remembered the advice he'd often given her about loosening up a little, when he was temporary manager of Housewares.

"I don't know—do you need one?" he bantered back at her. "I'll be happy to oblige."

She decided not to answer, afraid she'd say something she shouldn't. "You're here to escort me to lunch, I presume?"

"You presume correctly." He offered his hand to help her up from her kneeling position. Instead, she balanced herself on the shelf to stand up. "Do I detect a hint of repressed anger?" he said.

"I don't know—do you?" she sassed.

He skewed his mouth to one side for a moment, then seemed to regear himself and asked, "Do you like the Brasserie?" He was referring to the highest-priced restaurant of the department store's three restaurants, all located on the seventh floor.

"Of course," she said in a more genial tone.

"Fine. Let's go."

They took the elevator, crowded with holiday shoppers, to the seventh floor and walked the short distance to the Brasserie. Though there was a line of people waiting to be seated, the hostess, recognizing Charles, immediately found a table for them by a window that overlooked North Michigan Avenue. Jennifer felt a little embarrassed about getting such favored treatment.

After they'd ordered, Charles said, "So, what do you think of being chosen as our window lady?" His tone of voice was unexpectedly glum.

Jennifer drew in a deep breath and straightened the napkin on her lap. "Frankly, I'm not exactly thrilled. Why was I chosen?"

"Why?" He seemed taken off guard by the question. "Well . . . I forget why exactly. I left it up to the marketing people and the wardrobe and cosmetics experts. They got together, said they'd considered all the female employees and decided on you." He paused a moment. "Oh, yes, they said you had a slim figure, so you'd look good in the clothes they're selecting, and apparently Mr. James thought you had a nice bone structure. Someone in marketing commented that you had an air of intelligence and competence that would well represent our store."

Jennifer was dumbfounded by the compliments and also amazed. "You mean, you didn't choose me yourself?"

"*Me?* No! Though I was a little relieved when they told me you'd been selected."

So, Jennifer was thinking, he hadn't chosen her as a practical joke or to get back at her for previous skirmishes. Then she processed what he'd just said. "Relieved?"

He exhaled tiredly. "If I'm obligated to spend a week in the window with a woman, I'm glad it's turned out to be someone I—"

"What do you mean, *you're* going to be in the window?" she interrupted.

"It's not my idea, believe me. I argued with my dad about it for over a month—and lost. If my father weren't still on the mend from his heart attack, I might have had the gumption to say *no way!* Instead, I caved in."

"Really?" she said, incredulous that Jasper Derring would want his son, the store's new president, on display in such an undignified way.

"'Fraid so," Charles replied. "It's ironic, since the whole concept of a living window display was originally *my* idea."

She nodded. "I guessed that."

"The notion came to me one day when I was at home watching the angelfish in my aquarium. I ran it by my father that evening when Mom and Dad had me over for dinner. At first he shook his head. He said it sounded completely outlandish. Well, the next morning, Dad called me at my condo and told me he'd thought it over, and now he absolutely *loved* the idea. In fact, he thought it would generate even better publicity if *I* appeared in the window—Derring Brothers' new young president actively demonstrating the store's advertised personal touch."

Jennifer couldn't believe it. Had the heart attack affected Jasper's judgment?

The waiter came by and brought them wide-rimmed bowls of chicken and rice soup.

"I was appalled. Still am," Charles continued, picking up his spoon. "I almost wish I'd never thought of the idea, now that I've gotten roped into it. But Dad insists it'll be terrific publicity, and frankly, I'm willing to do *anything* to make Derring Brothers' Christmas sales the highest ever. I really do want that. It would finish off the year I became president with a bang. So, I've agreed to make a fool of myself in the windows for a week to get the publicity we need to generate the sales figures I want to see. I want Derring Brothers to be everyone's favorite department store."

As Jennifer observed the light of determination in his eyes, she couldn't help but think she was seeing a new side to him. She'd always had the impression that he was a fun-loving millionaire's son who thought life was a breeze. This desire to accomplish something important to him was admirable, she decided. She just wished she hadn't been selected to be a part of it. Maybe *he* had a good reason to make an exhibition of himself, but Jennifer didn't and was hugely reluctant to make one of *her*self.

She hesitated, then decided she must speak up. "I wish you success with the idea, Charles. But... I really—"

His eyes narrowed. "Look, believe me, I hate this as much as you. Don't tell me you're going to bail out on me in my time of need!"

She looked askance. "I just can't see myself being on display like some showgirl. It's not me."

"No, not like a showgirl," he said with irritation. "You haven't heard the whole concept yet." His eyes seemed to acquire a remnant of enthusiasm for his idea. He leaned toward her over his soup, the steam rising into his beautiful tie. "It's meant to be a representation of real life. We'll use all three Michigan Avenue windows. One will be set up like a kitchen, the second like a combination living room and home office, and the third like a bedroom."

"A bedroom?"

He smiled. "No need to be shocked. The display will show off selections of our bedroom furniture, draperies and linens, some of our workout equipment and...oh, yes, and books from our bookstore."

"And so—" she felt confused and flustered "—so what will we do...um...there? I mean, with all the people outside on the sidewalk staring at us?"

"Well, obviously nothing X-rated."

She felt heat in her cheeks and gazed out the window at Water Tower Place up the street. Then she looked back at him. "And what are we supposed to do in the other windows? Like the kitchen, for example. Am I supposed to pretend to be making your lunch?"

He shrugged. "Probably. We can do the food prepara-
tion together. The idea is that we look like a couple
spending their day enjoying a home completely furnished
with merchandise from Derring Brothers. I've got a team
working up a choreography, so to speak, of what we'll do
when. That's so each piece of merchandise gets a moment
in the spotlight."

"We're supposed to be a couple?" Jennifer asked,
picking up on something he'd mentioned and whizzed by.

"Yes. We're meant to look like married people. That's
the original idea I had. Of course, I thought we'd use professional models or actors. But Dad thought it would be
more homey if we used a store employee—and me."

"What if the newspapers make fun of the fact that we
aren't really married, though? We aren't nameless,
anonymous models. You're a Derring, the store's new
president—and it'll probably come out that I'm a store
employee. It might cause talk."

He made a nonchalant gesture with his hand. "I don't
see why. It's all for fun, an amusement for people to stop
and watch for a minute as they walk down the street. Even
if it does cause a little stir, so what? At this point, I don't
give a damn what the papers say about me, just as long as
they put it on the front page."

"But some reporter might start asking personal questions about us, about our personal lives. I'd find that embarrassing, wouldn't you?"

Charles ran his hand over his eyes. "Jennifer, the whole
situation is already embarrassing. I'm often a ham at parties, but I've never impersonated a department-store
dummy! It's too ridiculous a situation to take it all so seriously. My dad wants this, and we just have to go with the
flow." He paused and smiled at her in a brotherly way.
"Maybe this experience will be good for you. I kept try-

ing to loosen you up when we worked together. You're too
young to be so uptight."

Jennifer didn't particularly like his didactic manner. She
might have told him so before, but now that he was president, she decided she'd better not. Besides, she had other
things she needed to apprise him of.

"It's not only that I don't feel comfortable doing this,"
she said, moving her water glass to one side. "It's not appropriate for me to do it because of the man I'm dating."

Charles leaned back and tilted his head to one side. "I
saw you a few weeks ago leaving the store with a tall, dark-
haired guy with glasses. Is that . . . ?"

"Yes, he's Peter Bartholomew. He's an English professor at the U of I. I met him when he came in a few months
ago to buy a can opener as a wedding present for a friend.
We talked and he asked me out. We've been dating ever
since."

Charles nodded. "So, what's his problem?"

"Well, it's not *his* problem," she said with some testi-
ness. "It's mine, actually. He wouldn't approve of my being on display in a store window. He doesn't even think I
should work—" She caught herself before saying the word
here.

Charles's blue eyes took on a cold aspect. "You mean he
looks down on you because you're a saleswoman?"

"No . . . well . . . he thinks I should finish my education
so—"

"So you'll be good enough for him." He pointed his
spoon at her. "You're wrong. It's not your problem. It's
your stuffed-shirt boyfriend's."

"Don't call him that."

Charles studied her and shook his head as if with dismay. "I don't get you. You talk back to *me* readily enough,
but you're cowed by this guy. Why? Because he's a pro-

fessor? Do you think you're not good enough for him as you are? You should feel free to do whatever you want without fearing his disapproval. I say dump him!''

''Well, that's some advice!'' She'd grown angry at being described as *cowed*. ''You've never even met him.''

''I don't need to. I can see he's put a clamp on you, and I don't like it.''

''I don't have to look for your approval, either,'' she countered. Then she remembered that he was her employer. ''At least not on personal matters.''

To her surprise, Charles seemed to grow angry, too. His eyes carried a sharp light now and his mouth tightened. She'd never seen him angry. ''You're actually sticking up for a man who acts as if you're beneath him? Are you that in love with him?''

The question shook her a bit. She wanted to be in love with Peter and hoped she was. ''My romantic feelings are none of your concern.''

Charles lowered his eyes and pushed his bowl of soup away. ''You're right,'' he said after a moment. ''Your personal life is none of my business. It just ticks me off to think you're kowtowing to some egghead. You're too good for that.''

Jennifer felt surprised by his words. She wouldn't have expected him to have any particular regard for her. ''Thanks.''

He glanced up. ''So, you won't do the window thing?'' He looked impatient and disappointed.

Jennifer chewed her lip. ''I don't really think I'm suited to be in the spotlight like that anyway, even if I didn't have Peter to consider. For example, I don't like to wear makeup, and I understand Mr. James has been hired for that week.''

"Yes, he has. We've also lined up a hairdresser to do your hair. And we've got a whole array of clothes for you—day wear, sophisticated evening dresses, and luxurious nightgowns. I would think it would be fun for a woman to wear nothing but gorgeous clothes for a week."

"Nightgowns?" *Oh, God,* she thought as gooseflesh made the tiny hairs on her arms stand on end beneath her suit jacket. Peter would never, ever, approve.

Charles smiled. "Nothing see-through, I'm sure. You'll probably wear satin robes over them."

"F-for the bedroom display?"

"Of course."

"And what will you be wearing?" she asked.

His face went blank. "I don't know. I didn't bother to ask. Pajamas and a robe, I'd guess."

"And you don't think the newspapers would have a field day with Charles Derring, bachelor president of Derring Brothers, appearing in a window in his nightclothes with a woman who's his employee?"

Charles leaned his cheek on his knuckles, elbow on the table, and said, "It's not as if we were being discovered in some sleazy hotel room. It's a publicity stunt. Everyone will know that. There's nothing exploitive or secretive going on to be exposed. As my dad pointed out to me, I *am* considered one of the city's most eligible bachelors. He thinks this'll cash in on my reputation. I don't *like* it, but he's probably right."

"Well, what about me? My reputation?"

His blond eyebrows drew together. "You think your reputation would be compromised because you'll be seen in a store window with me in our pajamas? With, as Dad predicts, hundreds of people watching and news photographers taking our picture? That's going to make you a fallen woman? Nowadays, there's no such thing as a fallen woman anyway. It may make *you* sought after by every eligible guy in metropolitan Chicago. After Christmas, you'll be able to lose your stuffy professor and have your pick!''

The waiter brought them club sandwiches, but Jennifer couldn't eat. She felt thoroughly confused.

Charles studied her expression and his face softened. ''Look, I know how you feel. I'm full of reluctance, too. You're worried about your professor. Well, I haven't even had the nerve to tell my girlfriend about it yet—she'll probably laugh her head off! I'm sure we'd both rather be with our significant others than stuck with each other in a store window twelve hours a day. But you and I are *both* employees of this store, and unfortunately, duty calls. Will you think it over? I can give you till tomorrow, but no longer.''

She reluctantly nodded. ''All right,'' she said softly.

''I really hope you'll say yes.''

''But why?'' she pleaded. ''There are other women working at the store who are more glamorous than me and would jump at the chance. I'm not the only female employee who's thin, has good cheekbones and looks competent. Why not pick someone who *wants* to do it?''

Charles bowed his head for a moment. ''I started to tell you before that I was relieved when they chose you. Because you're about the only store employee I can think of whom I'd be able to tolerate being around twelve hours a day for a whole week.''

This amazed her. ''Why?''

''Well…'' He seemed to have to think about it. ''You're never boring, for one thing.''

Jennifer was surprised. Compared to his glittering debutante girlfriends, she would have thought he'd find her dull.

"And," he added with emphasis after another moment of thought, "you're not the type of female who would either be sucking up to me the whole time or trying to seduce me. It's not easy being rich and the head of a big company. Sometimes I feel like a target. But you're not the sort who has ulterior motives. Also, you treat me as if I'm an ordinary person. I like the way you level with me and talk back to me. I enjoyed the way we used to rib each other and pull pranks. It was like . . . like having a sister. I have a sister, but I don't see her much anymore since she left Chicago. I sort of began to think of you in her place. So I'd appreciate it if you would do this as a favor to me. Be the one to share the misery with me. Don't make me have to do window duty with some female I can't trust. Please?"

He'd made such a complimentary and surprisingly candid speech, Jennifer felt guilty now for creating a problem. "I'll talk it over with Peter tonight."

Charles drew in a long breath. "Okay. Just make sure, after you talk to him, that you're the one making the decision, not him."

"Of course." Jennifer had the nagging feeling, however, that that might be easier said than done.

After six, as Jennifer waited outside the main entrance of Derring Brothers, she thought over her conversation with Charles. The fact that she was uneasy about talking to Peter and that he might have undue influence over her decision had worried her all afternoon. Maybe Charles was right. Had she somehow become Peter's doormat? When they'd met, Peter had impressed her with his intellect, his seriousness about life and his profession, his refinement and his quiet manner. He was responsible and reliable, true to his word; in short, he was everything that she'd thought she wanted in a man, in a husband. Even more. She'd never hoped to attract someone with such a high level of education. But sometimes she felt inadequate around him, and she didn't like the feeling.

While she was mulling this over in her camel overcoat and red scarf, standing beside the store's main entrance in a freezing temperature, all at once she saw Charles come through the revolving door. He was looking straight ahead and didn't see her as he strode toward a black limousine that had pulled up to the sidewalk a few minutes ago. The limo driver got out to open the rear door of the long, highly polished vehicle. As soon as the door opened, a dazzling blonde appeared, complete with sparkling, low-cut evening gown and long chinchilla coat. She kissed Charles soundly on the mouth, then moved over so he could get in next to her. The driver sped them away moments later.

Well, Jennifer thought. *A new one for his collection.* Over the years, she'd caught glimpses of him with various beauties, usually blondes like him. It figured. He had the best cars, the best clothes, the best department store— though not the biggest. He wouldn't go out with anyone ordinary, would he? He'd have to have the best babes on the market, too.

Shame on you, Jennifer told herself. Just because the woman was beautiful and blond, she didn't deserve to be called a babe.

What was she doing thinking about Charles's women anyway? She had her own love life to worry about. As she looked to the south, she saw Peter approaching. She waved and he smiled back as he closed the twenty yards remaining between them. He stood well over six feet tall, and looked very masculine in his heavy winter overcoat. His brown hair was clipped close beneath his earmuffs; it looked as if he'd just gotten a haircut. When he reached her, he kissed her on the cheek, which was unusual. Peter did not like public displays of affection.

"How are you?" he asked. "You had me worried all afternoon by that phone call. What's going on?"

She told him the story as they walked up the street to Water Tower Place and went to one of the restaurants in the building. Later, over beef Stroganoff, she finished describing her dilemma.

"I consider myself a loyal employee. So on the one hand, I'd like to do what they want. But on the other, I'd feel totally out of place being a model in a window."

"Well, of course you would," Peter said with grim asperity. "The whole thing would be totally demeaning."

"Demeaning?"

"You're an intelligent young woman, Jennifer. You have a sense of decorum, a personal dignity, which is what I found so attractive about you when I met you. You're worthy of better things. Derring must not have much respect for you if he expects you to react like some wanna-be cover girl who only aspires to wear designer clothes and have her picture taken."

"He said they chose me because I look intelligent and competent," she told him.

"Of course you do. I'm glad they noticed. So why don't they find a more meaningful way to use your intelligence and competence than to put you in a display window in a nightgown?"

Jennifer couldn't seem to find an answer.

Peter reached across the table and took her hand. "This is just another example, the worst one yet, of what I've been trying to make you see—you don't have any future in that department store. Go back to college. Get your degree."

"In what?" she asked. "When I was in college, I changed my major three times in two years. I never did figure out what I wanted to do or be. That's why I quit and went to work. I felt I needed some real work experience to figure out what I wanted to do with my life. And when I started working as a saleswoman, I found that I was actually happy doing that."

Peter shook his head. "You couldn't be. You have far too much potential to be happy selling toasters."

"Peter," she said, drawing on her courage, "I think I should be the one to decide whether I'm happy or not."

"But, Jennifer, I don't think you know yourself well enough yet to decide that. You haven't had a chance to explore your capabilities to the degree you would if you returned to college."

"And you think *you* know me well enough to say that?"

Peter lifted his glasses as if to see her better. "My, we're in a rebellious mood tonight! You forget, I'm used to counseling students who require direction. I'm skilled at this sort of thing."

"You forget that I'm not one of your students."

"No, but you might be—if you went back to school."

She couldn't help but grin, though she felt unsettled inside. "If I were your student, you wouldn't be able to date me."

"I'd be willing to wait till you were graduated," he said, squeezing her hand.

"You're already willing to wait," she muttered.

"Hmm?"

"Never mind."

"No," he said, leaning forward with measured alarm. "What did you mean? I told you on our first date that I don't believe in jumping into a physical relationship. You seemed agreeable, even relieved. You told me you were tired of men who only wanted one thing."

"Yes, I was. Then. Oh, I don't mean we have to hop into bed just yet. But..."

"But what?"

She pressed her lips together in exasperation. Why did she have to spell everything out to him if he was so smart? Maybe nowadays he was wise to delay starting a sexual relationship, but she wished just once he would grab her and kiss her as if he was on the verge of losing control. It was as if he thought about every word before he said it, and every move before he made it.

She withdrew her hand from his, not knowing why, just wanting to. "Let's finish talking about the window display first."

"As far as I'm concerned, that's a closed subject. You absolutely should refuse to do it."

"Why?" she asked. "Would it embarrass you? Would your university colleagues laugh about it and tease you?"

"That has nothing to do with it," he said, adjusting his glasses again. She was only now realizing it was a nervous habit of his. Funny she hadn't noticed it before.

"What if I said I wanted to be in the window display?" she asked.

He looked at her sharply. "Are you being so rebellious on purpose? Are you trying to upset me?"

"Why is this all about you?" she asked. "I'm the one who would be in the window."

"I didn't say it was about me. I'm merely cautioning you that you'd allow yourself to be demeaned if you go along with it."

"And I think *you're* demeaning me, because you don't even care what I really want." The words flew rapid-fire from her mouth. "You're not helping me figure out my own mind. You're imposing *your* rigid ideas on me!" Jennifer caught her breath, barely believing she'd said what she'd said. But she wasn't sorry.

He stared at her mutely for a long moment, as if not knowing what truck had hit him. "I'm sorry if you think that of me. Believe me, I'm only trying to help."

"But you haven't been any help. I'll make up my own mind by myself, thank you. And," she added with a hint of recrimination, "I don't care what you think about it." She balled up her napkin and threw it on the table, then got up. "I'm going home now. I have to think things over."

Peter stood, looking shocked. "Wait, I'll drive you."

"No. Public transportation is good enough for a college dropout like me."

"Jennifer—"

She left the table and went out the door without looking back. When she returned to her small apartment in Elmhurst, she cried for a few minutes. Afterward, she felt relieved and good about herself. The only thing was, she still didn't know if she should agree to be in the window display with Charles or not.

At about nine-thirty, she was still thinking it over when Peter phoned. "I'm sorry if I sounded too much like your guidance counselor. I shouldn't have. I shouldn't treat you as a student. You just seemed so confused. I wanted to help."

"I know," she said, calmer now. "It's okay."

"You forgive me?"

"Sure, Peter."

"And what have you...decided?"

Something made her proclaim her answer before she even realized what she was saying. "I've decided to do it."

"Oh."

"And I hope you'll be supportive of my decision."

"I...ah...well, of course, I will. Of course. Certainly."

"Will you come by the window and wave at me?"

"I wouldn't miss it."

She heard the acerbic tone in his voice. But she didn't care. She felt like a doormat who had gotten up from the floor and dusted herself off. Maybe she'd wind up making a fool of herself, but at least she was her own person again.

3

It was 8:00 a.m., a week before Christmas, and too early in the morning for Jennifer to be reporting for work at Derring Brothers. But here she sat in one of the executive conference rooms on the department store's top floor, reached only by a special elevator. While hot rollers were cooling in her hair, Mr. James used every size makeup brush in his arsenal on her face. She tried not to blink as he applied eyeliner on her lower lid with a tiny wet brush, then smudged it with another little brush.

"Marvelous," he crooned. "I love to work on green eyes."

Mr. James was an elegant, slim man of medium height who always wore a turtleneck under a casual blazer. He reminded her of Fred Astaire in his later years, except Mr. James was blessed with a magnificent head of shining white locks. Christine, the hairdresser hired to coif Jennifer for the window promotion, had all but drooled over Mr. James's hair when they were introduced a half hour ago.

Jennifer felt outside herself, as if she were present in body but not in spirit. Indeed, both Christine and Mr. James treated her as an object while they hovered around her. Jennifer was merely the raw material they'd been given to transform into a glamour girl, and they'd gotten engrossed in the challenge. And it must *be* quite a challenge. She always wore her brown hair long and straight, pulled back with a ribbon or barrette. As for makeup, the most she ever wore was a bit of blush and lipstick on special occasions.

"Can you please go light on the eye makeup?" she asked, watching him dip into the mauve shadow again. There wasn't any mirror around in which to see herself, but she thought he must have put enough lavender on her eyes to paint a ship. "I don't want to look gaudy."

Mr. James chuckled. "Gaudy? Why would I make you gaudy? I want you to be so gorgeous, women will rush into the store and buy out the whole cosmetics department. Relax. Leave it to me. Look up."

He was applying mascara to her bottom lashes when she heard the door to the room open. She couldn't see who came in and hoped it wasn't Charles. The day after he'd taken her to lunch she'd told him that she would agree to be in the window display to please him, since he'd asked so nicely. But she'd made it clear she still wasn't thrilled with the idea. She might be in for some ribbing from him about the rollers in her hair and the makeup.

"Mr. Derring," Mr. James said, turning from her. Jennifer drew in a breath, steeling herself for some barb from Charles. "So nice to see you again. How was New Zealand?"

New Zealand, she thought.

"Beautiful. It's summertime there. Hated to come home." The voice was that of an older man. She managed to twist slightly from the position Mr. James had put her head in, and she caught a glimpse of Jasper Derring. Seeing him was a surprise, but then it occurred to her that perhaps he'd come for the 9:00 a.m. press conference

Charles was holding as a kickoff for the window promotion.

"I hope someday I can vacation there," Mr. James said, going back to work on Jennifer's face. "Spectacular scenery, I hear."

Jasper stepped up within Jennifer's view. She smiled and self-consciously murmured good-morning, not anxious for anyone to see her in rollers and a makeup cape.

Jasper winked at her and responded to Mr. James's comment. "Almost as spectacular as Miss Westgate."

"Doesn't she look lovely?" Mr. James chimed in, obviously proud of his work. "She has exquisite eyes. Excellent choice, sir, I must say."

Embarrassed at the compliments, and at being spoken of as if she weren't in the room, Jennifer also grew confused. She remembered that Charles had told her his staff had chosen her from among the store's employees. But Mr. James seemed to be saying that Jasper Derring had selected her. Maybe she'd misunderstood Mr. James's meaning.

"Don't look so doubtful," Jasper said, smiling as he spoke directly to her for the first time. "You aren't nervous, are you?"

"A little. I'm not sure I'll like being stared at all day."

"My dear, I'm sure you have admirers all day long as it is," Jasper said, the lines in his forehead deepening as he raised his eyebrows whimsically. He was an elfin man, even in his dark blue business suit and tie. "You just never notice them. You're one of those unsung heroines who quietly comes to work early each morning, does her job efficiently and without fanfare, and goes home late, leaving no loose ends. When I was president, I wished all my employees were like you. I was glad Charles got the opportunity to work with you in Housewares. I knew you'd set a good example for him."

Jennifer's jaw had slackened by the time he finished. She didn't know what to say, why she was receiving so much admiration from the retired president. He'd always called her by name and occasionally said a few words to her, but she assumed he behaved that way with all the store employees. "Th-thank you," she stuttered.

"Now, don't let Charles intimidate you when you're in the window with him this week," Jasper went on, raising his index finger. "Your head's just as good as his. In fact, it's probably screwed on better. Charles has lots of flash and dash. He's got innovative ideas—like this living display. He's the right fellow to take Derring Brothers Department Store into the twenty-first century. But he thinks life is a theme park, and he's always looking for a new roller coaster. He needs to grow some roots."

Jennifer squinted slightly, trying to discern the meaning in Jasper's dark, almost black, shining eyes. For a silly moment, she wondered if he was looking to *her* to somehow provide the fertile soil for the "roots" Charles needed to grow.

No, he couldn't possibly have meant that. She was just jittery and nervous and, as a result, confused. She wished she could go down to Housewares and open up her cash register as she did every morning, instead of sitting here having her face painted and making enigmatic conversation with the store's ex-president.

All these new expectations of her left her feeling a little helpless. She was beginning to wish she'd followed Peter's advice and refused the assignment—not because Peter was right, but because whoever at Derring Brothers had chosen her had made a mistake!

Jasper's mouth became an O as he seemed to study her expression. "Oh, my, I didn't mean to distress you." He patted her shoulder. "No, I want you to enjoy this week. I... I simply meant that you shouldn't be afraid—because Charles is your employer now—to put him in his place if you need to. It'll be good for him. I've always called him Charles, not Chuck or Charley, hoping that it would give him a keen sense of responsibility and personal pride. It hasn't worked." He smiled. "Maybe you'll have better luck."

Jennifer's head was swimming with Jasper's advice. "I doubt it," she said.

Jasper merely chuckled and said amiably, "We'll see. I'll leave you now and admire you again at the press conference."

"Will the reporters ask *me* questions?" Jennifer asked before he turned to go.

"They may."

"What shall I say?"

"Whatever comes into your head," Jasper replied. "I trust your judgment."

He walked out, leaving Jennifer in a daze as Mr. James eagerly went back to work on her eyes.

Charles cleared his throat as he approached the microphone. The room had been set up with fifty chairs, and most of them were filled. The reporters sat with notepads and tape recorders ready, while photographers at the back and sides of the room set up their videocams and still cameras. His father stood in a corner of the room observing. All that remained was for Jennifer to come in. An aid had just told him she was changing into her first window outfit and would be there in a minute.

This is going to be a great day for Derring Brothers!
Charles told himself as he stood in front of the arrayed
news media, growing enthusiastic at seeing such a good
turnout from the press. He was glad his dad was there to
appreciate it.

"Good morning!" he said to his audience as light bulbs
began to flash. "Let's begin now. Jennifer Westgate, the
Derring Brothers employee who agreed to do this crazy
thing with me, is on her way. You've all seen our ads, so
you know that beginning today, for the entire week before
Christmas, we're going to have what I call a living display
in our three Michigan Avenue storefront windows. If you
haven't already, I hope you'll go out and photograph our
beautiful show windows, which have been made to look
like rooms in an elegant home—a home that's been decorated *exclusively* with Derring Brothers merchandise!"

The reporters seemed passive and wore jaded expressions on their faces.

Undaunted, Charles continued with energy. "Likewise,
Miss Westgate and I, who will live in the windows all week
from ten to ten, will be clothed in a marvelous selection of
Derring Brothers garments." He glanced at the door when
he noticed it open. Behind the photographers standing at
the back, he caught a glimpse of a woman entering with
Mr. James, who gave him the okay sign with his hand. "I
believe this is Jennifer now—"

Charles stopped short when he saw her emerge from
behind the photographers as she approached the front.
Was it her? My God, it was! A strange sense of awe came
over him. She looked gorgeous. Not that he'd ever thought
she was ugly. But... he'd never thought... she just had
never been the splashy type. She was always too sensible
for glitter and glamour. An unexpected rush of anger
whisked through him, replaced by a breathless numbness.

How was he going to spend a week in the windows with this... this distraction? Where was good old dependable, down-to-earth Jennifer?

She was wearing a shimmering blue pantsuit with a big belt that made him realize how tiny her waist was. She'd always worn two-piece suits with boxy jackets to work. But her outfit was nothing compared to her face and hair. Her long brown hair was all voluminous and wavy now and swung rather provocatively around her shoulders as she walked. And her face, which used to look like a choirgirl's, now looked like a cover girl's. Her eyes, particularly, had a rare, almost mystical beauty. He'd never noticed they were so wonderfully green.

When she reached his side, she looked at him, at the audience, and then at him again, her magical eyes perplexed. And then he remembered he was in the middle of a press conference and was supposed to be saying something.

"Um... this is Jenn—Miss Westgate. Jennifer Westgate. She ordinarily works in Housewares. But she'll be with me all week... in the windows."

The reporters were chuckling, some silently, some audibly, as if genuinely amused. Charles didn't know why. He also had forgotten whatever else he'd intended to say for his opening statement. Thinking quickly, he suggested, "Why don't we open it up for questions now?"

A woman reporter in the second row raised her hand. "What will you two be doing in the windows?" she asked.

This was followed by laughter throughout the room.

"That's a good question," Charles responded in a serious tone, ignoring the laughing. "Our staff has drawn up a schedule for us to follow. For example, in the kitchen we'll be preparing, then eating, breakfast—a different dish every day made with an assortment of appliances from

Housewares. I believe that's probably one of the reasons Miss Westgate was chosen for this assignment, because she's familiar with how they all operate."

"*You* didn't select Miss Westgate?" a man in the back shouted.

"No," Charles replied. "I left that up to a team of experts I assembled to choose which of our employees would be best suited for the assignment."

"Then," the same man in the back shouted, "who chose *you?*"

Charles smiled. "I meant to cover that in my opening statement. Since this promotional display was my idea, my father, Jasper Derring, who is here today—" Charles pointed out his father, who was still standing quietly near the corner of the room "—suggested that I ought to be the man in the windows. It's a good way to introduce me, the new president, and continue the tradition of personal attention and service our store is famous for. When the store president is the live mannequin in the window, it should project to the public an up-close-and-personal touch you won't find at any other department store." Charles was glad to have gotten that point across, but he had the feeling the reporters weren't particularly interested in the store's image. They seemed to have something else on their minds.

A woman to the left raised her hand. "Are you married, Mr. Derring?"

"No," Charles replied.

"And is Jennifer married?" the same woman asked.

Everyone looked at Jennifer, who replied with a soft no.

A male reporter in the front row stood up and asked, "Is there a romance between you two?"

Charles was thrown off guard. "No, not at all."

Jennifer stood next to him, wordlessly shaking her head. She began chewing her lower lip and looked self-conscious.

"Let's hear from Jennifer," someone in the back shouted.

Jennifer wet her lips. "I'm dating someone and I believe Mr. Derring has a lady in his life, too. So, there's no romance between us, nor will there be."

Charles exhaled with grateful relief. Thank God Jennifer knew how to handle the question. Why would the reporters think there was a romance between them?

The reporters were silent for half a second, momentarily hushed by Jennifer's all-encompassing response. Then a woman halfway back raised her hand. Charles pointed to her.

"You seemed rather surprised, or maybe stunned is the word, when Jennifer came into the room," she said, standing up. "What was going through your mind when she walked in?"

Charles felt baffled, first because he didn't know how to respond, and second because he couldn't figure out why the reporters were asking such personal questions. Suddenly, he had a vague recollection of Jennifer pointing out to him, that day at lunch, that the media might make an issue of the two of them being unmarried, yet posing as a married couple. He quickly gathered his wits.

"I was simply awed by how beautiful she looks. Doesn't she?" he asked them. "It just shows what Derring Brothers' clothing and cosmetics departments can offer a woman. Jennifer is always attractive, but now she's been transformed into a . . . a mysterious, sultry siren. I'm impressed! Aren't you?"

As he looked over the audience, he could see cagey expressions on some of the reporters' faces, as if they wanted to use a certain angle in their reporting and were trying to figure out what questions to ask to get that angle. Charles reluctantly acknowledged to himself what they were looking for—a romance between him and Jennifer. For the sake of potential sales, he realized he ought to try to play along. "After spending a whole week with her, I may find myself calling on Derring Brothers' bridal registry to print up wedding invitations!" he proclaimed with a big smile.

As the murmuring and light-bulb flashes increased, he glanced at Jennifer. Beneath the sophisticated makeup, she gave him a typical Jennifer expression, one eye squinting at him with distrust and her mouth quirked in puckish amusement. The reporters clearly loved what he'd just dished out, but she wasn't buying it for a second. And in this artificial atmosphere of lights, publicity and momentary chaos he'd helped create, Charles found that reassuring.

It was late morning when Jennifer was allowed to take a break from window duty and go to the ladies' room. There, in the mirror, she saw for the first time what Mr. James and Christine had made of her. The sight was something of a shock, but after a second or two, a not altogether unpleasant one. She did look stunning. No wonder Charles had appeared so dumbfounded when she'd walked into the press conference. Maybe it was also why he'd been behaving as if he didn't quite know what to say to her as they began their life together as window models.

She looked like someone else—no, that wasn't right. Studying herself more closely, she decided she looked like herself, but it was as if she were standing on a pedestal in a shaft of glowing moonlight with wind billowing out her hair. Her face had a subtle radiance from the makeup and her eyes carried a shadowy glow. It was all fake, but she had to admit it looked darn good. She wondered what Peter would think when he saw her this way. He'd promised to come by after he finished work in the late afternoon.

But that was hours and hours away, she thought drearily as she left the ladies' room to go back to the window. She and Charles had spent their first two hours on display making waffles in a waffle iron and then pretending to enjoy eating them at the cozy maple table in the kitchen setup. Neither had been very hungry. It was just as well—now they had to prepare lunch and eat that. For some reason, their communication wasn't faring any better than their appetites. Charles seemed nervous around her, and she wasn't sure why. She'd never made him nervous before. Certainly he knew she hadn't taken his comment about wedding invitations seriously.

Or, maybe he didn't know. Maybe she ought to reassure him that she took his comment as fodder for the media. After all, she'd been the one who had predicted the reporters might take that tack.

As she went through a small, camouflaged door and stepped up into the kitchen display window, she saw Charles, already back from his break. Through the giant floor-to-ceiling windowpane, she could see that the sidewalk crowd had grown larger over lunch hour. Charles, wearing a burgundy sweater and slacks, his scheduled attire, came up to her.

"Ready to make the club sandwiches?" he asked, a crease between his blond eyebrows.

"Oh, I just can't wait!" she replied with flippant enthusiasm. "How about you?"

She smiled at him, but his face fell back into the worried, preoccupied expression she'd seen all morning. He didn't answer.

"Charles," she said as they walked over to the white kitchen sink, set into imported Italian tile, "what's the matter? Every time I look you in the eye, you resemble a deer caught in headlights. It's not like you. I thought I would be nervous, but instead, you are.''

Charles nodded. ''The press conference didn't go as I'd planned and...''

So she'd guessed correctly. ''Look, I know we're not going to order wedding invitations when this is over, so don't worry. I understand that your comment was just a joke, to give the reporters what they wanted to hear.''

''Well, I knew *that* from the way you squinted at me,'' he told her in an impatient tone. ''We both know there's nothing between us and never will be—as you put it so well—so...so, that's not the problem.''

She leaned against the sink and studied him. ''So, what is?''

He spread his hands. ''I don't know. This is just... different from what I expected.''

''Do the crowds gaping at us bother you?'' She leaned around him to check, and sure enough, a dozen passersby had their faces to the window, watching them. One waved at her, so she waved back. Charles turned, smiled, and did the same.

He faced her again. ''It's not as bad as I thought. I'm getting used to it. I'm a born ham.''

''That's what I thought.''

He almost laughed. ''You know, you sound like you, but you just don't look like you. I...I can't get used to...this.'' He gestured toward her hair and face. ''It threw me the minute I saw you, threw the whole press conference askew, and it still throws me. Do you have to look like you were just voted glamour model of the year?''

Now she was ticked. ''Look, it wasn't my idea to get myself gussied up like this! I told you, I told Mr. James and anyone else who would listen, that I don't like to wear makeup. But did anyone pay any attention? No! And now you're complaining—"

"Okay, okay." He raised his hand, palm out, in a defensive gesture. "You're right. It's not your fault you had to wind up beautiful. I just can't put the two together, your old personality and this...this face. I'm comfortable with the personality, but your face and hair and figure are a damned distraction. I can't get used to it. For some reason it...makes me angry."

"Makes *you* angry? Why?"

He shrugged. "How the hell should I know? It's just a...a change that I didn't expect. I thought we would be supportive of each other doing this display thing together."

"And we can't now, because I look too good?" she asked, trying to understand.

"I know it doesn't make any sense," Charles admitted.

She sighed and straightened up from leaning against the sink. "Well, at least *that's* normal. You never do make much sense."

He laughed and seemed to relax, the crease in his forehead vanishing. "I'm glad that underneath you're still your normal self, too. Give me a few more hours. I'll get used to your fabulous face, I promise." He rubbed his hands together, as if acquiring new energy. "Let's make lunch. What did they give us for the club sandwiches?"

"Let's see," she said, opening the tall, sparkling white, state-of-the-art refrigerator. She began taking things out and putting them on the counter. "Bread, lettuce, mayo, some kind of cooked poultry meat." She opened the cellophane. "Is it chicken or turkey?"

He took it from her. "Looks like turkey. What's that?" he asked as she drew out a clear plastic container. "Ham or bacon?"

She opened the container. "Canadian bacon."

"Good," he said with exaggerated relief. "Ham makes me self-conscious."

Her shoulders shook with laughter. Maybe this would be fun after all.

In the late afternoon, after they'd changed into their formal attire to share some already-prepared hors d'oeuvres in the living room window, Charles found that his nervousness had inexplicably returned. He wore a black tuxedo and Jennifer had put on a turquoise beaded evening gown with a high neckline and long sleeves. The sparkling dress covered her demurely, yet clung provocatively to every curve. Charles never knew Jennifer had such curves. And now his heart was beating funny again.

He wished he could get a grip. What was the matter with him? He'd seen sexy women before. He'd dated them all his life—was dating one now. But, for some reason, it just didn't seem right to him that *Jennifer* should be sexy. It unsettled him.

As she sat next to him on the plush leather couch, spreading caviar on a cracker, she crossed her legs, and suddenly a long slit in the skirt, which he hadn't noticed at first, opened at the side, revealing the most beautiful legs he'd ever seen. The men in the crowd outside the window looked as if they were almost salivating. Charles wanted to tell her to go inside and put on something else, something less showy, something . . . dull. Like she used to wear. And then he had to remind himself that he was the one who had arranged for her to look this way.

"Caviar?" she asked, offering him the cracker she'd spread.

"No, thanks!" he said, his voice testy.

She looked mildly taken aback. "We're supposed to be enjoying ourselves, or at least acting as though we are."

You're enjoying yourself too much! he wanted to tell her. He stiffened his lips to keep from spitting the words at her. She was right, of course. Why had he come up with this ridiculous idea anyway? He wished the week was over already.

In a huff, he took the cracker from her and popped it into his mouth. While he was chewing, he suddenly spotted a very familiar face among the gallery of people peering through the window at them. Lushly wrapped in chinchilla, she was blond, smiling and gorgeous, and she blew him a kiss.

"Delphine!" He leaned forward toward her. "Thanks for coming!" he shouted, hoping she could hear him through the glass.

She nodded and her smile grew even more effervescent. "How are you?" she asked, mouthing the words slowly. He could barely hear her muffled voice.

"Great!" he replied.

"Delphine?" Jennifer said.

"My...friend," he explained. "She's a model. She promised to stop by." He turned back to the blonde on the other side of the glass. "Dinner tonight?" he shouted. "Meet you at ten?"

Delphine gave an exaggerated affirmative nod, as if she were looking forward to more than dinner. Charles appreciated her response. Somehow, after a strange day, he was glad to be able to look forward to getting back to his normal life. He'd been dating Delphine for almost three months now. She was fun-loving, adventurous, flirty, everything he enjoyed in a woman, besides being a knockout. She came from a wealthy family, but had turned to modeling as a career. Her family didn't approve, probably because she was especially sought after for swimsuit and lingerie shoots. That didn't surprise Charles in the least. She had a fantastic body and enjoyed showing it off. More power to her, Charles had always thought.

His energized thought pattern was scattered by a sardonic feminine voice beside him.

"Are we supposed to engage with our onlookers to this degree?" Jennifer asked coolly.

"She's a friend. I'm just saying hello."

"Right," she acquiesced with a little sigh. "More caviar?"

"No."

"Sure?" she said, interrupting again as Delphine was trying to tell him something else. "It's all we get to eat to tide us over until we're off duty at ten."

"Huh? Okay," he said, taking another cracker. He looked back at Delphine, who was repeating what she'd been trying to say.

"She says you look very handsome in your tux," Jennifer told him in a tedious manner. "She mouths every word so sensuously, how can you miss what she's saying?"

"Because you interrupted," Charles snapped back. He poured himself some champagne from the chilled bottle on the oak coffee table in front of them, and thanked Delphine for her compliment with a silently gestured toast to her.

He almost spilled his glass, however, when Jennifer suddenly bounced on the cushion beside him, waving eagerly at someone in the crowd.

"Peter!" she exclaimed. "I'm here! It's me!"

Charles recognized the tall man she was waving at. He'd seen her meet him after work. Peter, who was near the center of the window, two people away from Delphine, seemed to be looking around as if confused. When Jennifer kept waving at him, he looked at her again—he'd passed her over before. Then, as the realization hit that she, indeed, was Jennifer, Peter's eyes widened enormously, the effect intensified by his glasses. He looked absolutely shocked. Charles could sympathize with his feelings, though he instinctively disliked the man without ever having met him.

Jennifer bowed her head for a moment in response to Peter's reaction.

"Don't let him burst your balloon," Charles told her. "Every other man at the window is slobbering over you."

She looked at Charles. "Thanks," she said dourly. "Peter will probably never respect me again."

"That's his problem," Charles said, then drank some champagne. "Have a glass of this and just ignore your learned sourpuss."

After Charles poured a second glass then handed it to her, he and Jennifer paused in unison as they observed a new development outside the window. Peter and Delphine seemed to be introducing themselves to one another. The two middle-aged women who were standing between them had apparently walked off while Charles was preoccupied pouring the champagne. This left Peter and Delphine standing next to one another, pushed together by the crowds on either side of them.

"Why is Peter talking to *her?*" Jennifer said, setting her glass on the table.

"I suppose they must have noticed each other trying to communicate with us," Charles said. "I think I saw Delphine say hello first. She's the outgoing type."

"I can imagine," Jennifer said dryly. "Well, one thing's for sure, those two have nothing in common."

"Right," Charles agreed with a chuckle. "Except significant others to visit in a store window." He quietly watched as Peter and Delphine continued to talk. "What could they be saying to one another?"

"Beats me," Jennifer replied. "I wonder if Peter even knows what she's saying. He seems fixated on her mouth. Does she always have that provocative way of moving her lips?"

Charles hooked his forefinger over the upper edge of his shirt collar. It felt tight. "That's just how she talks," he said lightly, trying to hide his irritation, remembering it was the first thing he'd noticed about Delphine when he'd met her at a party. It had instantly turned him on. Who would have thought a cold fish like Peter would react the same way? Stuffy professors must have hormones, too.

"Now they're laughing," Jennifer said. "I think they've forgotten us."

"No," Charles insisted, thinking Delphine couldn't possibly have been distracted by a fish-eyed professor, even if he was tall and imposing. "They're just being ... polite."

"She's flirting with him," Jennifer said.

Charles studied the situation. "She flirts with everyone. It's just her style. He's the one who's responding."

"He is n—" Jennifer didn't finish. "He couldn't be. He hates cheap women."

"What do you mean *cheap?*" Charles objected. "Why would I go out with anyone cheap? She comes from an old Gold Coast family."

Jennifer shrugged. "What's Dolly Parton's joke about herself? It takes a lot of money to look as cheap as she does? That could be Delphine's motto."

"How would you know?" Charles said. "Style was never your strong point." He glanced at her, her new dazzling appearance, and realized his remark no longer applied.

"High fashion was never my ambition," she said. "And why are we talking about me? What about Samson and Delilah out there?"

Charles and Jennifer both looked out the window again, staring at the new acquaintances still getting to know each other with such apparent enthusiasm. Perhaps it was the feeling of two pairs of eyes burning into them that suddenly made Peter and Delphine turn from each other and look back into the window. Instantly, both appeared self-conscious and embarrassed. Delphine gave Charles a frivolous smile and shook her shoulders as if she didn't know what had come over her and didn't mean to ignore him. Peter, meanwhile, was straightening his tie and apparently composing himself. He gazed at Jennifer with contrition.

Delphine blew Charles a kiss, mouthed the words "See you later" and took off—but not until she'd shaken hands with and said goodbye to the professor.

Peter similarly signaled to Jennifer that he'd meet her at 10:00 p.m. and walked off in another direction.

"Well, that was interesting," Jennifer said with ironic understatement.

"Oh, don't worry about it. I'm not," Charles lied. "Besides, if it's glamour that Peter likes, he's got it in you now. Use it," he advised in a tight tone of voice.

Jennifer shook her head worriedly. "That's what I don't get. He obviously didn't like *me* dripping with makeup and sequins, but he seemed taken by Delphine's bleached hair and chinchilla coat. I thought he believed in animal rights, too!"

"She got it after being photographed in it for an ad," Charles said. "She's not what you'd call politically aware."

Jennifer sniffed. "Her interests are more centered on herself, I imagine."

Charles studied Jennifer with new eyes. "I didn't know you could be so catty."

She looked self-conscious. "It must be the mauve eye shadow Mr. James used on me. It makes my eyes more green."

"With jealousy?" Charles asked, amused.

"I suppose," she admitted. "I don't like the feeling."

"I'm sure when Peter sees you a few hours from now, up close and personal, he'll be just as impressed with you." Charles was trying to reassure her, but he didn't feel sure himself. He didn't know what bothered him more—that Delphine might be attracted to the professor, or that Jennifer was already so attached to the guy. Charles wondered if *he* should start wearing glasses. Thick lenses certainly seemed to turn on the women in his life.

He paused to reexamine that last idea. It threw him just slightly. He'd never consciously thought of Jennifer as being a woman in his life before.

About an hour later, Charles and Jennifer changed into their scheduled attire for the bedroom window. His pajamas were of blue silk and were partnered with a matching velour robe. He was only mildly embarrassed to be wearing them in the window with people watching. Except for a few chest hairs that showed, he was all covered up.

Jennifer, however, seemed rather self-conscious in her pale pink satin robe. Underneath, showing beneath the robe's lapels, which fastened at her waist, was a long satin-and-lace nightgown. It was V-cut, and Charles caught a glimpse of cleavage. He murmured that she looked great, wanting to reassure her, and then glanced away. Exercise equipment was set up in one corner, so he went over and began doing some leisurely bench presses. He used similar equipment at home to keep in shape. Jennifer sat up on the bed and read a book. They passed the remaining few hours until ten in silence while evening shoppers paused to stare.

Charles was glad to have something to do so as not to have to deal with Jennifer. Instead, he tried to think about what he would say to Delphine when he saw her tonight. Should he make light of her long introduction to the professor? Was Delphine trying to make him jealous?

Charles found he couldn't keep his mind on Delphine. He kept stealing looks at Jennifer, who continued to read in a regal, sad sort of silence. He had the feeling Jennifer's life would be changed because of this window promotion, and Charles felt responsible. Maybe that was why she made him feel so unsettled. Maybe he simply felt guilty for insisting she take part in something she didn't want to do. He wanted to be able to just tease her again about little things, about letting her hair down and having more fun, the way he used to. But that easy, bantering manner they used to have with each other was changing, and Charles wondered if they would ever have it back again.

After Jennifer had changed out of the nightgown into her own tan suit, she hurried toward the door where she always met Peter after work. Thank heaven Peter hadn't stuck around to see her in pink lace and no bra. The wardrobe woman had refused to let her find something more demure.

She went out just before the security people locked the doors. Peter was waiting outside on the sidewalk. A light snow was falling. He seemed distracted and a little uptight.

"So," she said lightly, taking his arm, "what did you think?"

"Of what?" he asked cautiously.

"The display. Of me in the display."

"Oh. Well, I was surprised. You look different with your hair that way and the makeup. But you seemed to apply yourself to the task ably."

"Thank you," she said, disappointed with the compliment. "I guess you like the old me better."

He gazed over her face as they walked. "It's not that you don't look pretty. I'm just used to you without all the fuss and bother."

"You seemed to like Delphine, though. And she has lots of fuss and bother." All designed to make men *hot* and bothered, Jennifer thought to herself.

"But it suits Delphine," Peter said. "She's just one of those young women who have a flair about them."

Jennifer nodded. "You certainly seemed attracted to that flair."

Peter smiled, rather self-consciously. "I, like every man, have a baser side to myself. I can be attracted to a ball of fluff now and then, too."

"But you don't like my looking like a ball of fluff?" she asked.

"You *don't* look like one."

"I mean now, with the teased hair and eye shadow."

Peter shook his head. "No, you still don't. You look like a competent woman who went to the wrong beauty parlor, where they mistook you for a Miss America contestant."

Jennifer mulled over that comment for a few moments and then decided to give up trying to interpret what Peter thought. But she needed to know where she stood with him in their relationship.

"Are you still upset with me for agreeing to be in a display window?"

Peter seemed to consider his answer before speaking. "No," he said carefully. "I'm happy if you're happy."

"Does it embarrass you? There were lots of photographers taking our pictures in the window throughout the day. I'll probably be in the newspapers."

"You were on the TV news at six," Peter told her.

"I was?"

"Yes, they showed a portion of the press conference. You were standing next to Charles Derring. He was saying something about printing wedding invitations after your week together was over."

"Oh," Jennifer said, her heart sinking. "He didn't mean that."

Peter shrugged, apparently unconcerned. "Of course not. He said it to create a stir for the reporters. That was obvious. Why would he marry *you?*"

Jennifer turned her head to look at him. "I'm such a bad catch?"

"Not at all. But he's clearly a shallow show-off. That's why he's got Delphine. She's nothing but a trophy to him. I feel a little sorry for her."

Jennifer drew in a breath, wondering why they were talking about Delphine. "So why wouldn't he see anything in me?"

"Because you're intelligent. You have a sense of propriety. A man who's only looking for fun, for a good time, wouldn't choose you."

"And what about you, Peter?" she asked, her breath caught in her throat. "Do you still choose me?"

Peter paused in his steps. His expression grew sensitive and he smiled. Slipping his arm around her, he said, "Of course I do. Let's go find a place that's open and have a sandwich.''

They did exactly that. And then he drove her home. He kissed her at the door and left, wiping her lipstick from his mouth with a handkerchief as he walked back to his car. She'd forgotten—Peter hated lipstick.

4

The next morning in the kitchen display window, Charles was standing at the counter scrambling eggs in a glass bowl with a hand-held electric mixer. He'd put on a long cook's apron over his sweater and pants. The apron was a green-and-red plaid. His resourceful wardrobe staff had selected it from the Housewares department for a holiday effect. Next to him, Jennifer, wearing a similar apron with a Christmas tree printed on its red background, was chopping onions. They were supposed to be making seasoned scrambled eggs for breakfast. So far, other than deciding how to divide up the work, they'd said little to one another. Charles decided to take the plunge.

"So, what did Peter say to you last night?"

Jennifer looked up sharply, her eyes red and watery. "About what?"

Charles turned off the mixer. "Was he angry? Did he say something nasty to you?" he asked with concern.

Jennifer laughed, wiping her eyes with the back of her wrist. "No, he was his usual composed self. Why would you think he might be nasty to me?"

Charles hesitated at stating the obvious. "Well...you're crying."

She looked askance and sighed. "It's from the onions."

"Oh. I didn't think of that. I'm glad things went okay. You seemed worried last night about how he would react to your new look."

She lifted her shoulders in a little shrug. "He seemed to accept it, but thought it didn't suit me." Her chopping got a little more energetic. "He said I looked like a competent woman who'd gone to the wrong beauty parlor where they'd mistaken me for a Miss America contestant."

Charles pondered the words for a moment. "What's wrong with being mistaken for a Miss America contestant?"

Jennifer laughed wryly as she dabbed at the corner of her eye with a kitchen towel. "I don't know. And I always thought Miss America contestants looked pretty competent anyway. Peter has his own arch way of seeing things, though." She leaned toward Charles, turning her face upward. "Did I mess up my eye makeup? Mr. James spends so much time on it, I'd hate to ruin his work." There was a trace of sarcasm in her tone.

Charles found himself blown away by the beautiful green eyes staring into his, looking even more dramatic with their glossy sheen from the onions. "Looks fine to me," he said, trying to sound nonchalant. "He'll probably give you a touch-up at break time."

"I'm sure he will," she agreed as she grabbed a green pepper. She pushed aside the board with the onions. "You might tell your staff not to give us any more onions to chop."

"Right. I will." Charles turned on the mixer to continue beating the eggs, his mind preoccupied. "So...did Peter say anything about meeting Delphine last night?"

"Yes." Jennifer whacked the green pepper in two with one stroke of her knife. "He had lots to say about her."

Charles switched off the electric mixer again. "Like what?"

"He said that, like all men, he has a baser side and he can be attracted to a ball of fluff now and then."

Charles jumped on the information. "So he admitted it! He *is* taken with her."

"Yes, he more or less did." She glanced up at Charles as if pondering whether she should say more.

"What else did he say?"

She continued to hesitate.

"Come on, spill it," Charles urged. "We might as well know what we're dealing with."

"He described you as a 'shallow show-off,' and he said Delphine was nothing but a trophy to you. He said he felt sorry for her."

Charles was dumbfounded. "*Sorry* for her? Your professor must have a screw loose! Sorry for *her!* If anything, she looks on *me* as a trophy."

Jennifer kept on chopping. "Good, I'm glad you realize that," she murmured.

"Huh?"

She glanced up. "I said I'm glad you see that."

Charles suddenly felt argumentative. "You think I'm Delphine's trophy? How did you arrive at that?"

She gestured with her knife. "It's sort of obvious. I might not have put it in those words, but when you said it, it sounded right. She looks to me like a pricey party gal who likes to show off what she's got, and now she's got the young president of a famous department store to show off. You're probably in the same category as that full-length chinchilla she likes to flaunt."

"You're absolutely wrong! That's the most misguided thing I ever heard." Charles turned on the beater again, wishing he actually felt the conviction he'd put into his defense of Delphine. A nudging voice inside was telling him Jennifer was right on the mark. He didn't want to hear the voice and drowned it out by raising the mixer to a higher speed. Soon the beaten eggs were splashing over the side of the bowl.

Jennifer shrugged. "Okay, maybe I'm wrong. I don't even know her. But you asked, so I told you what I thought." She looked at the bowl he was working over. "Charles, you're going to have those eggs all over the counter. There won't be anything left in the bowl to cook!"

Charles turned off the mixer. "Who's hungry anyway?" he muttered.

Now Jennifer was hesitant. "You're upset. What's wrong?"

"Nothing."

"Charles, I told you about my conversation last night with Peter. What happened when you talked to Delphine?"

Charles took the beaters out of the mixer and rinsed them in the sink, which had been supplied with a limited amount of water. "Nothing in particular."

"What did she say about Peter?" Jennifer urged. "I told you everything Peter said to me about their meeting. Now it's your turn."

Charles put the rinsed beaters aside and exhaled. He turned to Jennifer. "All right. You might as well know. She was very impressed with your professor. She said, 'Why is a man of his caliber going out with a little shop girl?'"

"Little shop girl!"

"Yes. Sorry. That's what she said. Delphine is the type who's well aware of her rank in society."

"So why is she a model if she comes from such a wealthy family?"

"She's rebellious and enjoys upsetting her parents. Her family probably wouldn't approve of Peter, either, because he's not wealthy. Is he?"

Jennifer shook her head.

"That's what worries me. Her family likes me. They wouldn't be happy at all if she started seeing Peter, so that might be all the incentive she needs to pursue him."

"Doesn't she go out with a man because she *likes* him? Does she always have an ulterior reason?"

Charles leaned against the counter. "It's not as though she thinks it all through. She's impulsive. She became attracted to me at the yacht party where we met because I knew how to steer the boat—the owner let me take over the controls for a while. I have a yacht of my own. She was impressed with my prowess at that and...at other things."

"What other things?"

"Never mind," Charles said. He'd never been accused of being a bad lover. But he wished women appreciated him more for himself, for the basic human being he was. He'd grown disenchanted with his playboy image. "I'm wealthy and—as you pointed out—I'd made news becoming the youngest president of a Chicago department store. She likes high-profile men."

"So why would she be attracted to Peter? He's not wealthy or high profile. Just to upset her parents?"

"I'm not sure," Charles replied. "Maybe he's got a different sort of clout. He's a highbrow type, isn't he? Respected as an intellectual, no doubt. He's probably even written a book or two."

Jennifer nodded. "Yes, he has. That's why I was attracted to him and flattered that he saw something in me. He's refined. Tall. Authoritative. Almost like a...a father image. Some women are attracted to that.'' She looked down self-consciously.

''Why?''

''Well, if a woman had a father who was working all the time and didn't pay much attention to his daughter, she grows up looking for the male nurturing she didn't get when she was a child. That's my story anyway. It's only last night that I began to realize that's probably why I'm attracted to Peter.''

Charles was amazed at Jennifer's insight into herself. ''Is your dad still living?''

''No, both my parents are gone.''

''I'm sorry. It's good you're figuring yourself out. But I'm afraid that theory wouldn't fit Delphine. She was spoiled by her daddy from the day she was born. Maybe Peter's just a new sort of conquest for her.''

Jennifer was shaking her head. ''What do you see in her, Charles? You describe her as spoiled and looking for men to conquer. What's the appeal, if you're just another notch on her bedpost?''

The question annoyed Charles. ''I probably chose her for the same reasons she chose me, in the beginning. I like blondes—I admit it. I like showy, flirtatious women. They're fun. They're challenging.''

''What's the challenge?'' Jennifer asked, her brows drawn together.

''Attracting her and winning her, when every other man in the room wants her, too. Holding on to her while she makes eyes at other men, luring her back when she looks like she's about to stray. You have the woman every other man longs for. It's a way to one-up the men around you. It's a . . . a male thing.''

Jennifer rolled her eyes. "Well, if she's trying to stray to Peter, then this should be just another fun challenge for you to keep her."

Charles blinked. "Yeah, you're right." But he knew he was getting tired of the game. He was thirty-one now. He had a department store to oversee. Free time for dating strategies was no longer available. He needed a steadier sort of life now. He'd been sort of hoping Delphine might be ready to settle down, too.

"And for your sake, and mine," Jennifer continued, "I hope you meet the challenge and win."

He listened to her affirmation and felt strangely off center for a moment. "Right," he agreed, absently pouring the eggs into a frying pan. And then he said, "For your sake? You mean, you really want to hold on to your professor?"

"Yes."

"Even though you said he's serving as your father figure?"

She shrugged and bowed her head, her long curled hair falling forward over her shoulders. Charles felt an odd pang in his abdomen. For a moment, she looked like a lost little girl.

But then she looked up, and the wry adult humor he saw in her beautiful woman's eyes accosted him. "Maybe I'm hoping my sensational new look will turn Peter into a lover with a capital *L*," she told him.

The statement made Charles's mind reel. He didn't know why, but he couldn't think straight for the next few minutes.

He burned the eggs, onions and all.

Late in the afternoon, when they were in the living room display having hors d'oeuvres and champagne, Jennifer grew nervous, wondering if Peter would come to see her again. The dress they'd given her to wear this evening, a long hunter green velvet gown with a satin sash, bared her shoulders but not her cleavage. She thought it looked elegant and classy and hoped Peter would be impressed. The hairdresser had pinned up her hair into an elaborate French twist, and she liked that, as well.

Charles, who was spreading crackers with a cream cheese and spinach mixture, seemed quiet and anticipating, too. She guessed he was wondering if Delphine would show up. They'd passed the afternoon amicably enough, joking now and then and waving back at the window watchers who waved at them. Charles enjoyed mugging for little children, who laughed at him as they held on to their mothers' hands. It was a side of him Jennifer hadn't seen before. She was glad when a newspaper photographer took a photo of him making a funny face for a little girl through the window. A photo like that would give the store and Charles a pleasing public image. Though Charles seemed to be having too much fun to even notice the photographer.

But the enjoyable afternoon was ending and both had lost their humor, it seemed. Jennifer wasn't looking forward to the evening. She had an odd feeling that something consequential was going to happen.

"He's back," Charles said quietly, spreading another cracker.

Jennifer looked up from her reverie. Indeed, there Peter stood at the middle of the window, directly in front of the couch on which she and Charles were sitting. Peter gave her a jaunty smile, as if he was in a good mood—or at least pretending to be. She thought he looked unusually handsome. He'd left off his earmuffs and instead put up his coat collar to protect his ears from the frigid outside air. And he'd nonchalantly thrown a long black wool scarf over his shoulders, so that the ends hung down the front. This was a new touch. Jennifer had never seen him use a scarf before, much less wear it in such a stylish way. She wondered if he'd studied the clothing ensemble on some mannequin in a men's store.

After saying hello, she motioned to his scarf and said, "Very nice!"

He nodded back, looking pleased.

She stood, ostensibly to brush crumbs off her velvet dress, but then she turned to one side and then the other, modeling the gown for Peter. "Like it?" she asked.

Peter eyed her up and down, smiled, and gave her a thumbs-up sign with his gloved hand.

"Will you sit down?" Charles said. "You don't have to make a spectacle of yourself."

"Grouchy, grouchy," Jennifer said, sitting next to him again. "Just because Delphine hasn't shown up yet to gush over you..."

"She'll probably gush over your mad professor instead. He's sure looking spiffy tonight! Is that for your benefit, or is he *hoping* to run into Delphine again?"

"I don't know," she said, pouring herself some champagne. And then she remembered something. "As he was driving me home, he asked me if Delphine was going to be there every night. He said it as if wondering aloud, but I had the feeling he was hoping I'd know. I told him I had no idea."

"You're going to have to learn to keep your man on a tighter leash," Charles said.

"How?"

"How?" he mimicked. "You must have some feminine wiles for that sort of thing."

Her chin rose. "No, I'm afraid I don't. I suppose I should take some instruction from Delphine. She seems to have you pretty well tethered."

"What's that supposed to mean?" he said, turning on her.

"Does she spend as much energy worrying if you're still her man as you do wondering if she's got a roaming eye for someone else? If there's a leash between you two, you've got the collar end and she's got the lead."

Little sparks flared in Charles's blue eyes. It was the second time she'd seen him angry. "There isn't any leash between Delphine and me. We're two adults who let each other lead their own life-style."

"Fine," Jennifer replied. "It's the same with Peter and me."

"Baloney."

"Let's not discuss each other's love lives, okay?"

"Fine with me."

He downed his champagne and poured another glass. Jennifer glanced out the window at Peter and caught him looking up and down the sidewalk. She'd hoped he would be wondering what she and Charles were talking so animatedly about, but it seemed he wasn't. What did it take to hold Peter's attention? she wondered. Obviously, an elegant evening gown and hairstyle weren't enough.

And then, from the corner of her eye, Jennifer caught sight of a dramatically long, luxurious, pale fur coat winding its way through the crowd. Above the large collar was a matching head of hair. The beautiful face was smiling, not at Charles, but at Peter. She tapped Peter on the arm to say hello. He turned instantly, and the biggest smile Jennifer had ever seen appeared across his face.

"Are you seeing what I'm seeing?" Jennifer said quietly to Charles.

"Yup," he said, staring at them, too. Delphine turned from Peter to wave at Charles and blow him a kiss. Charles blew one back. Then she turned to smile at Peter again.

"I may be sick," Jennifer muttered under her breath. "She's flirting with two men at once!"

"No time to be sick now," Charles said. "Let's fight fire with fire. Try to keep Peter's attention and I'll try to keep hers."

Jennifer spent the next twenty minutes trying to follow Charles's advice. She waved to Peter, shouted questions at him. Would he come by to pick her up afterward? Where should they go to eat? Where did he get the scarf? He answered them all, but was constantly being distracted by the blonde next to him. Meanwhile, Charles kept drawing Delphine's attention with questions and quips. She'd answer him using her provocatively mobile lips to mouth each word and smile. But then she'd always turn back to the professor and joke and smile at him. Jennifer was amazed at the strange aspect in Peter's eyes. Even through his dignified glasses, he looked dazed and earthy. His usual cerebral air was vanishing. Apparently, the baser part of himself was making another appearance.

Jennifer grew frustrated and tired of trying to keep his attention, and by the long sigh she heard from Charles, she suspected he was getting fed up, too. It was then they got the cue, whispered by a staff person at the back door of the display window, that it was time to change clothes and switch windows.

"Guess we have to go," Jennifer said, uneasy about leaving Peter with Delphine unchaperoned. "I hope they're still here when we get back."

Charles looked incensed. "What, do you think they're going to run off together while we're gone?"

"No, not really," Jennifer said. "Peter told me he'd meet me at ten, and Delphine's supposed to meet you. I just hate to leave them alone without us to monitor them."

Charles got up from the couch. "We have to do more than monitor them. You haven't been doing a very good job of keeping Peter's attention."

"You haven't kept Delphine's attention, either," Jennifer countered, rising from her seat, too.

"I know." Through the window, Charles eyed the pair who were engaged in conversation. "What does she see in him? I'd better clue them that we'll be back in a different window, or they'll never notice."

He walked over to the windowpane, stood in front of Delphine, and knocked to get her attention. All the other spectators watched Charles curiously, but Delphine and Peter didn't turn until he'd knocked four times.

"Back in fifteen minutes," he said to her through the glass. "In the next window. Okay?"

"Okay," she said and blew him another kiss.

Meanwhile, Peter glanced at Jennifer and motioned that he'd move to the next window to see her. Jennifer smiled, glad he'd gotten the message, too. Maybe he and Delphine were simply bored and that was why they talked to each other so much, she told herself as she began to walk out of the display window to change. When Charles caught up with her, she said to him, "Maybe they're talking to each other because it's so hard to talk to us through the glass. It's probably tiresome just to stand out there in the cold and watch us."

"The other people in the crowd don't seem to get tired," Charles said. "Some of them stand and gawk by the hour."

"That's true," Jennifer admitted. "But still, Peter is highly intelligent and needs more stimulation than watching a window display for a long time, even with me in it. So he needs to talk to someone.''

''I think I know what kind of stimulation he needs,'' Charles said sarcastically as they stepped out of the window.

Jennifer didn't want to ask him what he meant and was glad they had to separate then to change clothes.

In the dressing room, Jennifer was outraged to see the black lace nightie waiting for her. It looked like something out of one of those catalogs she always threw away. She took off her dress and slipped the black lace over her head. It showed a daring—for her—amount of cleavage and the lace barely camouflaged her nipples. She didn't even bother to ask if she could wear something underneath, knowing what answer she'd get. She slipped on the matching long robe, but as a cover-up it did little. Its long sleeves covered her arms, but left her chest exposed.

Self-conscious and embarrassed, she went to the bedroom display window. She found Charles waiting by the small entrance door, wearing black silk pajamas and a black velour robe. He looked ... unbearably handsome, Jennifer thought, swallowing. ''Delphine ought to like you in that,'' she said in a light tone of voice.

Charles took an all-encompassing look at her and then averted his eyes. ''If Peter's half a man, he ought to break through the window to get to you.''

At his words, Jennifer felt an unexpected little thrill rush through her. She wished Charles would look at her again, and the wish surprised her.

Then, Charles did look again. ''You—'' he shook his index finger at her ''—you aren't supposed to look this sexy—I mean—this good. It's not ... fair.'' He seemed perturbed with himself. ''I mean, this isn't how I intended

Derring Brothers to be represented. It's not supposed to be like a Vegas show—"

Jennifer gasped. "Do I look that indecent?" She tried to draw the sides of the flimsy robe closer together. "Should I take it off and see if they'll find something else for me?"

Charles studied her and seemed to grow restless. "No. No, I'm...overreacting. It's not that revealing. If Delphine were wearing it for a photo shoot, I wouldn't think twice. It's just...on you...I don't know. You're not the type who would wear something like that, so it seems inappropriate."

Jennifer remembered Peter's remark last night. *You have a sense of propriety. A man who's only looking for fun, for a good time, wouldn't choose you.* She felt confused. How did *she* want to look? she asked herself.

"Well, then," she told Charles, "I'll have to adopt a different attitude while I'm wearing it, so it doesn't seem so out of place on me."

"How do you mean?" Charles asked, looking worried.

"I'll take a page out of Delphine's book and talk like this," she said in a high voice, making her lip muscles exaggerate each syllable. "Does black lace suit me now?" she asked, leaning toward him and blowing him a kiss.

Charles's face grew stern and his eyes darkened in a fiery way. "Stop that!"

Jennifer was taken aback. "I was just joking."

"Save it for Peter. Maybe it'll work on him."

"Delphine talks like that, and you like it on her."

"You are not Delphine," he told her. He took her by the shoulders and gave her a shake. "Be yourself!" Then, as if for the first time realizing he was touching her, he let go. He wet his lips and seemed to compose himself. "Come on, we've got to man the display window."

"One of us is 'womaning' the window," she contradicted as she followed him into the bedroom setup, again trying for humor.

He turned and gave her a tense little grin. "Save the language lecture for later. We've got our work cut out for us. Look at that." He gestured toward the window.

Delphine was leaning her shoulder against the glass, crushing her beautiful fur coat, while Peter stood facing her, looking down at her with engrossed eyes.

"Think they missed us?" Charles quipped darkly.

Jennifer was shaken by the sight. She'd never seen Peter so fixated—on anything. "You think maybe they're falling in love or something?" she asked. "Even Delphine seems sort of serious. She's not flirting now. They look like they're deep in conversation."

"How could they be falling in love already?" Charles asked, studying them with amazed eyes.

"Love at first sight," Jennifer replied.

"I don't believe in that. Never happened to me."

"It's never happened to me, either, but look," she said, gesturing toward the couple who had yet to turn and notice them. "Something significant seems to be happening."

Charles shook his head. "What would they see in each other that would make them fall in love?"

"What did Arthur Miller and Marilyn Monroe see in each other?" Jennifer said, feeling her heart sink. She was losing Peter. She could sense it was inevitable.

"I never did figure that one out. Come on, we can break this up. I'm not giving way to a nearsighted egghead!" Charles walked up to the window and banged on it, near the spot where Delphine's fur coat was pressed against the glass. "We're back again!"

Both turned. Peter's expression was a rigid mystery. Delphine smiled at Charles but looked reticent, almost sad.

Something heavy duty is going on out there! Jennifer thought. She waved to get Peter's attention. He instantly lowered his eyes, and she knew he'd seen her. Then he looked up. His gaze was regretful, but meaningful and determined, too. She sensed he was trying to communicate to her with his eyes, since they couldn't really speak at the moment.

Jennifer already knew his message. He was leaving her for Delphine. She could see he was so taken with Delphine, it had overridden his normal nature. He needed to act on his desires. He couldn't help himself. Jennifer was amazed. It was obvious this was something he'd never experienced before—and he *wanted* the experience. She almost envied him. Tears filled her eyes.

Peter's forehead creased with concern. He mouthed the word *Sorry.* Jennifer nodded. She really did understand, even though she was losing him. She turned and set her hand on Charles's arm. He was in the midst of shouting through the window to Delphine, who was smiling, yet withdrawing from him by taking a small step backward.

"You said you'd meet me at ten," Charles was reminding her.

"I can't," Delphine said. "Something's . . . come up."

Jennifer realized Peter was much more straightforward with her about what was going on than Delphine was being with Charles. Perhaps Delphine hoped to hang on to both men.

"What could have come up in fifteen minutes?" Charles asked.

Delphine pulled her coat closer around her. "Sorry, darling. I'll explain later."

"How about now?" Charles insisted.

Jennifer tugged on his arm. "Give it up, Charles," she said softly.

"What do you mean?"

"It's no use. I think they're . . . going to be with each other tonight."

Charles narrowed his eyes at her. "Are you crazy?"

"No. I could tell from Peter's look."

"Are you saying they're dumping us?"

"Shh," she said, tugging Charles away from the window. "Let's try to take this like adults. You've had lots of women friends. You'll find someone to replace her in no time."

She sat down on the bed and urged him to sit next to her. He did, looking shocked. "How do you know?" he asked.

"From Peter. He looked at me sadly and said he was sorry. I'm sure he means to leave me for Delphine."

"Well, Delphine hasn't said that to *me*. Peter may think he's in for a hot time tonight, but Delphine hasn't indicated she's going off with him."

"She said she can't meet you," Jennifer reminded him.

"She probably just remembered something she had to do. She can't explain everything through the window."

"Charles—"

He emphatically shook his head. "I could accept Delphine dumping me for some football player or some actor or some other millionaire. But a dusty professor? Give me a break!"

Jennifer and Charles looked out the window again. Peter had taken hold of Delphine's hands as if he was urging her to leave with him. Delphine seemed to be resisting, though her eyes were only for Peter. Then she seemed to be imploring him to wait a moment before turning back to Charles.

Instantly, Charles slipped his arm around Jennifer's shoulders.

"What are you doing?" Jennifer asked.

"Making them jealous."

"You think that'll work?" she asked, incredulous.

"Delphine is the proud type."

Indeed, Delphine seemed to be surprised to see Charles cozying up to her. Jennifer decided to play along for Charles's sake. She had a feeling Peter wouldn't care at this point, but someone as fickle as Delphine might.

Delphine smiled slightly. She pointed her leather-gloved finger at them, first at Charles and then at Jennifer. She mouthed to Charles, "You and she? Together?"

Charles nodded and pulled Jennifer closer. He slipped his other hand around the front of her waist. Jennifer was beginning to feel embarrassed. And yet there was something heady about being so close to Charles, feeling his body heat. She was glad they were only playacting. She wouldn't know how to handle the situation otherwise.

Peter whispered something to Delphine. She nodded and then looked back at Charles. "You're really happy with her?"

Charles took hold of Jennifer's hand and kissed it, then glared at Delphine with silent defiance.

Delphine's posture slumped as she sighed—with relief, Jennifer thought. "Good luck, darling," Delphine shouted to Charles and blew him a grand final kiss. "Be happy!"

"What!" Charles dropped Jennifer's hand and watched, looking stunned as Delphine took Peter's arm. Peter mouthed goodbye to Jennifer, and he and Delphine left the window to walk off together into the lights of the city night.

"Guess the jealousy thing backfired," Jennifer said, choking down the lump in her throat.

Charles got up and tried to get a last glimpse of them out the window. "I don't believe it. She was so hot for your staid professor, she left me to go off to bed with him!"

"You don't have to spell it out so bluntly," Jennifer muttered, feeling humiliated now. She hadn't let herself think about what the couple were going to do together. But she knew Charles was probably right. She could see the helpless desire in Peter's eyes. He'd never looked at Jennifer like that.

"You might as well face the truth," Charles told her glibly. "The guy could hardly keep his pants zipped."

"Don't say that," she chided him. "I thought Peter handled the situation he found himself in with as much dignity as he could."

"You're sticking up for him? He just dumped you to get into the nearest bed with my girlfriend, and you think he was dignified?"

"I think he was hit by a bolt of lightning. He couldn't help himself." She shook her head. "I wish it had been *me* that he felt that way about, but it wasn't."

"Well, if you would have been more attentive to your sex life, he wouldn't have strayed," Charles said heatedly, pacing in front of her, oblivious to the remaining crowd outside. Their audience watched with riveted curiosity, as if they knew something was going on.

"We never had a sex life," she said with a tired sigh.

Charles turned and stared at her. "You never...?" A sharp new light came into his eyes. "No wonder he was so hot for Delphine. He was overdue." The anger in his tone seemed to have disappeared. After a moment, he sat down next to her on the bed again, but at a little distance this time. "How come you never slept with him?"

"Because I don't rush into sex and neither did he—until now," she said with irony. "So he and I waited by mutual agreement. And . . . I don't know . . . somehow we just never got around to it. He . . . didn't seem anxious to. He even told me that I wasn't the type of woman a man would choose to have fun with. He claimed to like me because I was the more serious sort. But, when push came to shove, I guess he liked the flashy, sexy type after all—Delphine.''

Charles stared at her, looking baffled and intense. ''I think he's nuts.''

She laughed. ''You chose Delphine for the same reason. Why is Peter nuts for being attracted to what you also like?''

Charles didn't seem to know how to reply for a moment. He stared at Jennifer as if he wasn't sure what he liked anymore. ''But I'm the type who fits with a woman like her, and you're the type who should have someone more reserved, like him. Sure, he's attracted to her now, but how will they feel the morning after?''

''That's a good question,'' Jennifer agreed. ''You think she might want to come back to you?''

''I don't know.'' Charles almost sounded as if he didn't care anymore. ''What about Peter?'' he asked more carefully. ''Will he want you back after he's had his wild fling?''

Jennifer shook her head. ''I don't think so. If he's about to experience passion, I don't think he'll go back to what he had with me, even if it doesn't work out with Delphine. Our relationship was all cerebral. Actually,'' she said slowly, with great deliberation, ''I don't think *I* would want to go back to it. I'd like to experience what they're having tonight—a mad, impetuous love encounter.''

Charles looked at her with disapproval. ''Jennifer, this doesn't sound like you at all. You must be upset. You've lost your boyfriend and you're feeling low. Don't go out and have a rebound affair with some guy. You could wind up feeling even more mixed up.''

"I don't think I'm mixed up," she contradicted. "I think I'm finally beginning to work out what it is I want in my life.''

Charles shook his head. "No, Jennifer. I think maybe these sexy clothes are . . . are getting to you. You're a nice, proper, levelheaded young woman. Don't change because your boyfriend runs off with a bouncy blonde and you're feeling left behind. The right man will come along for you. You don't want to change into some…some beguiling sex kitten. Who knows what kind of men you'll attract? It's dangerous! Just stay who you are. Trust me on this.''

Jennifer felt annoyed. "Now you're taking a fatherly role with me. I just got rid of one guy who did that, and you're—''

Charles's eyebrows shot upward. "No, I'm not! I certainly don't think of myself as your father, believe me. But remember, I did say I felt like your brother. Well, this is just a little brotherly advice.''

"I don't want to be your sister, either!" Jennifer didn't really know what she wanted from Charles—she just didn't like his advice, that's all.

"Well, pardon me," he said. "I'm just trying to help. You don't seem to be yourself.''

"I'll be the one to decide who myself is, if you don't mind!''

"Okay, forget I said anything." He waved his hand in the air flamboyantly. "Go and flaunt your cleavage to all the men staring at you in the window. Do a striptease!''

Jennifer rolled her eyes to the ceiling. "What's with you? Why are you saying all these strange things to me? Why would I do a striptease?''

"Because you want to be sexy like Delphine.''

"Even if I did, what's wrong—?"

"Because you're not like that!" he declared sharply. "You were chosen for this project because you appear competent. Your IQ should look higher than your bra size. The wardrobe people may have misguidedly put you in flimsy nightgowns, but as your boss, I expect you to conduct yourself with propriety."

"If I had a fling with a new man, I'd do it on my own time, not in the store window," she argued back.

"Don't sass me, young lady! I own this place and I can fire you for insubordination—like that!" He snapped his fingers at her.

"Go ahead!"

Charles stared at her a long moment. He seemed to be reining in his unleashed rage. Why was he so angry? she wondered.

Finally, he said, "We're both upset now. I'll think through your status with Derring Brothers tomorrow. For now, you're not following what we're supposed to be doing." He drew a piece of paper out of his robe pocket and opened it up. After glancing at his watch, he said, "It's nine o'clock. One hour to go. You're supposed to be reading in bed. I'm supposed to be exercising. Just like last night. So, let's follow our directions, shall we?"

"Yes, sir!"

He got up and went to the exercise equipment. She stretched out on the bed and grabbed a book. Was he really going to consider firing her? she wondered as she turned the book right side up. He thought she was acting strangely—well, what about him? He'd all but gone off the deep end! She'd never seen him threaten anyone's job before. Maybe he was really in love with Delphine, and this was how he was dealing with the shock of her leaving him.

Well, that was his problem, and Jennifer had her own feelings to sort through. If Charles wanted to fire her tomorrow, fine. She'd just do what Peter had always advised her to do and go back to college. Maybe Peter was right. Why did she ever think she had a future at Derring Brothers anyway?

5

The next morning, after Mr. James and Christine had done her makeup and hair, Jennifer changed into her assigned outfit, a long green sweater with matching leggings. As she made her way through the store to the kitchen display window, she saw Charles walking toward her in white athletic shoes. They'd dressed him in a navy sweat outfit with a wintry snowflake pattern printed on the top. He looked so casual, it was hard to believe he might be about to fire her.

"Good morning," he said.

She wasn't sure whether he sounded cool or merely formal.

"Morning. Well, am I fired?" She didn't like beating around the bush, and with Charles it wasn't necessary.

He took a hesitant little breath. "No."

"How come?"

He smiled at her oddly. "Were you hoping to be fired?"

"No. But you were so annoyed with me last night. I'd just as soon not stay here if I'm such a disappointment to my employer."

He studied her with amused absorption. "You *are* my employee, yet you always know how to put me in my place. You look at me without even blinking those big green eyes, as if daring me to fire you. You're never deferential like the others. How come?''

''I was there the day you ripped the seat of your pants, remember?''

''And whose fault was that?'' He pointed his finger at her. ''I ought to at least reprimand you for your sassy defiance.'' He put his hand down. ''But I don't seem to find myself doing that.''

Jennifer bowed her head for a moment, not sure what to make of this conversation. Then she looked up. ''I suppose you have a right to reprimand me,'' she told him honestly. ''I do talk back to you a lot.'' And then she remembered his father telling her she *should* talk back to his son. She became discombobulated by a sense of déjà vu, though she'd never had this conversation with Charles before.

''It's because we got to know each other when we worked together in Housewares as if we were on the same rung of the ladder,'' Charles said.

''No. In my mind, you were always the owner's son—though you didn't tend to act like it.''

''And last night,'' he continued intently just as if he hadn't heard her, ''we both went through our personal crises together, since we each lost our ex to the other's ex. So we have a little history together, and it alters the normal employer-employee relationship. It would be hard for me to fire you even if I wanted to. You're indispensable in Housewares. My father thinks so highly of you, he'd kill me if I let you go. And—my main reason—if you left, someone else would have to do window duty with me for the rest of the week. I wouldn't like that... for the reasons I told you when I talked you into this.''

Jennifer wondered why he felt the need to explain all his thought processes to this degree. It seemed to indicate that he regarded her as a friend with whom he could be honest. She relaxed and felt relieved. "I'm glad I'm not fired, then."

They began walking together toward the window. She swallowed and glanced up at him hesitantly. "I got a call early this morning from Peter."

Charles's head turned. "You did?"

"He said he and Delphine have decided to spend the holidays together at a place she has at Lake Tahoe. He's done with classes, so they're leaving tonight."

Charles laughed without humor. "She wanted *me* to go there with her, but I told her I couldn't because I had to be in the window display. Guess I was easily replaceable, wasn't I?" He shook his head incredulously. "I don't understand Delphine at all. Did he say anything to you about her?"

"Just that he was sorry to have so abruptly broken off with me and hadn't meant to hurt me, but...that the moment he'd looked at Delphine, he was lost."

"Lost?"

"That was the word he used. He said he'd never met anyone like her. And—" Jennifer sighed "—he mumbled something about losing his sense of direction and finding himself—" She stopped, hating to finish the story.

"Go on."

Peter's description stuck in Jennifer's throat, but she made herself repeat it. "'Awash in ecstasy.' That's what he said—regarding what happened between them after they left the window, I assume."

"Good grief! And she felt the same way?"

"Apparently. She invited him to Tahoe."

Charles mutely nodded.

"Is she a particularly good lover?" Jennifer asked out of intense curiosity.

Charles stared at her, his face a bit heightened in color. "What kind of a question is that to ask?"

Jennifer felt acutely embarrassed. This was not a question she should have asked her boss, especially after they'd just discussed their employer-employee relationship. "I'm sorry. I don't know what I was thinking, asking you that."

He chuckled. "I know what you were thinking. You want to know what brand of sex has suddenly gotten Peter glued to Delphine. She and I had a hot relationship at first. But lately it seemed as if either she or I were too busy—" He stopped short, looking annoyed with himself. "To answer your question, yes, when she's hot, she's hot. But I predict she'll fizzle out on him sooner or later, whenever she loses interest."

"For Peter's sake, I hope she doesn't."

"Why?"

"Because he'll have had a grand passion and then be left adrift, always looking to replace what he'd experienced with her. I'd rather see him be happy."

"You seem to have a fixation lately on 'grand passion.' I told you last night, it doesn't sound like you. You were always down to earth and practical."

"Maybe I'm tired of being that way."

"You're beginning to really worry me," he said as he opened the small door for her to enter the window display.

She went to the refrigerator for milk and pulled out pancake mix from a cupboard. "But you were the one who always told me I was uptight, that I should loosen up a little."

Charles took the carton of milk from her. "Yes, but you don't want to get too loose. You shouldn't go from one extreme to the other."

"Why not?" she asked, pushing the metal beaters into the electric mixer. "I'd like to know what it feels like to be swept away by an intense emotion."

"You might find yourself in a strong current and get washed down the river into the sea," he warned.

As she measured out pancake mix and dumped it into a glass bowl, she laughed ruefully. "Oh, don't worry so much, Charles. I just *wish* it would happen. It probably never will. Just as you've said, I'm too uptight. To give in to a 'grand passion,' a person has to give up control and yield to their emotions. I've never been a risk taker. People who are down to earth and sensible feel uneasy in strong currents. I'd probably head for shore the moment I felt a tug downstream." Tears filled her eyes as she poured milk into the mix to make a batter.

"Are you okay?" Charles asked.

"Sure." Jennifer blinked hard and willed herself to regain her composure.

In only a moment, she was back in control. Self-restraint was her strength. But she was beginning to realize that it might also be her downfall.

Two days later at noontime, Charles studied Jennifer as she ate her lunch. They sat at a small round table in the living room display window eating the turkey club sandwiches they'd made for themselves before leaving the kitchen display. Someone in the crowd outside the window waved, and Jennifer smiled and waved back, looking quite happy, even vivacious. They'd dressed her in a cream cashmere sweater today, and she looked—well, soft and cuddly. Charles glanced at his sandwich plate, feeling his thoughts straying again and trying to quell them.

It was no use. He might as well admit the truth to himself. He was beginning to desire her—Jennifer, his "sister," the epitome of the wholesome girl next door. He'd always liked women who were flashy, extravagant and a tad on the wild side. He'd always preferred blondes. Why was he having these unquenchable urges to take Jennifer in his arms and feel her against his chest, crush her dark hair in his fingers, kiss that mouth, and drown in those green eyes?

The worst time was in the evenings, when she wore some sexy nightgown in the bedroom display. Last night, he thought he'd go nuts. He hated the men outside who gaped at her with gleams in their eyes, and he wanted to tell her to cover herself with the bed sheets while she read her book. But he also had the strong desire to crawl under the covers with her.

Charles shook his head a bit to shoo away the memory beating there and took another bite of his sandwich.

"Is something wrong?" Jennifer asked.

"Huh? No. No. What would be wrong?"

"I thought maybe you weren't feeling well. Your face looks a little flushed or something."

He took a sip of his cold drink. "I'm fine."

What a lie. He'd never felt quite like this before, all inside out and upside down, not quite sure which way was up anymore. But at least he was beginning to acknowledge and accept this new, uprooted state of mind he found himself in. He'd been trying to deny his unexpected feelings toward Jennifer ever since she walked into his news conference looking like a woman to die for. All the strained silences, the strange conversations they'd been having, the curious feeling of relief when Delphine dumped him, the moments of quiet happiness, like now when they ate lunch together in front of onlookers as if they'd done this all their lives—all these mysteries made sense, now that he realized he was sexually attracted to her. And that, at least, gave him some peace of mind. For a while there, he'd thought he was going crazy.

But now what? Should he act on his desire for her? Jennifer was his employee. It wasn't a good idea for that reason alone.

Charles knew that major detail wouldn't stop him, though. What made him hesitate was Jennifer. How would she react? Would she respond or level him with one of her one-liners? Jennifer was the only woman he'd ever met who made him feel at a loss sometimes, who actually made him nervous. He knew, more acutely now than ever before, that she could demolish him with one quip, one word. He used to like the challenge a woman presented, but at the moment, he felt a little overwhelmed by her. He had no idea what she would do or say if he attempted to carry their friendship to a different plateau. But he had to try.

As he pushed his partly eaten sandwich away, Jennifer said, "Are you sure you're feeling all right? You're not devouring your food the way you usually do."

"I decided I need to lose a few pounds. I've . . . gained a little."

"Really? The way you pump iron every night, I'd have thought you'd have worked off any excess fat. You look very trim."

Indeed, Charles had worked hard on the exercise equipment every evening—to keep his mind off Jennifer on the bed. He raised his shoulders in a deliberate nonchalant shrug. "You know what they say—you can't be too rich or too thin. Well, I'm rich enough, but I decided I ought to work on the other."

She laughed. "Charles, the saying is 'A *woman* can't be too rich or too thin.' I don't think it's supposed to apply to men."

Feeling a tad demolished, Charles gazed up at the track lighting in the ceiling. "I stand corrected. If you're done with your sandwich, we have a tree in the corner we're supposed to start decorating."

"Yes, sir. Ready for action," she replied dutifully.

Charles couldn't help but wish that the action she was ready for wasn't decorating a Christmas tree. He repressed the thought and got up. She joined him as they opened up the box of lights and ornaments the department-store staff had left for them. The tree had been set up last night after closing time.

Charles took out of his pocket the daily schedule of activities his assistant had given him that morning. "Let's see," he said, opening it out. "We do the lights now, and the ornaments after we change at break time."

"Okay." Jennifer picked up a string of lights and straightened it out. She handed the end to Charles to place at the top of the ten-foot tree. As they wound the lights around the tree, they bumped against one another once, then again. Charles felt hot under his pullover sweater the third time he felt her back brush against his chest as she moved to reach another branch. All at once, she tripped slightly on his foot and briefly lost her balance. He slipped his arms around her waist to steady her, pulling her close to him without even thinking.

He felt her go still in his embrace. She was aware of him, of his arms around her—he could sense it in her silence. It was one of those timeless moments he'd heard about, as if the earth had paused in its orbit for a millisecond. Charles had never experienced such a moment before, not with Delphine, not with anyone. He stopped breathing.

"I'm all right now," she said, her tone light.

"Sorry my foot got in your way," he muttered as he let go.

"That's all right." She didn't look at him and went on with her work as if nothing had happened.

But Charles was very aware that something *had* happened. His racing pulse proved it. Things had definitely changed and there was no going back. This was fine with Charles—every fiber and cell in his body was anxious to move forward. And fast.

At break time, Jennifer headed for her dressing room. She changed into the strapless red velvet evening gown the wardrobe staff had selected. Her fingers were tremulous as she zipped it up the back. She'd been disconcerted ever since she'd lost her balance and found herself in Charles's arms. She'd felt something tangible between them, something odd—it was as if he wanted her in his arms. It threw her so much, she didn't know what to do, so she pretended it hadn't happened.

Was Charles attracted to her? She was nothing like his former girlfriends. Yet she'd caught him now and then gazing at her, especially in the evening when she was on the bed reading. Whenever their eyes met, he'd look away and do another bench press. She'd been wondering what that was all about, and now she had the Christmas-tree incident to file away and figure out.

Maybe she was mistaken. It just didn't make sense that he would be attracted to her in *that* way. He'd said more than once that he thought of her as his sister.

But if she wasn't mistaken, then she didn't know what to do. How should she respond? How did she feel about him? She'd never thought of him as a potential lover.

Lover? The word that had popped into her mind echoed and made her back straighten. Why hadn't the words *boyfriend* or *new man in my life* come to mind? Even they sounded farfetched. She'd just lost Peter and was still recovering. Wasn't it too soon to be attracted to someone else? Especially Charles. Why had she come up with the word *lover?* Was that what she unconsciously wanted Charles to be?

The question almost made her panic and she put it out of her mind. No, it was much safer to assume that she was mistaken in thinking that Charles was cozying up to her physically.

After having her makeup touched up and her hair restyled into an upswept do, she returned to the window. She went through the small, hidden door, then walked through the larger doorway that was part of the living room setup, to make the display window look more like an actual room.

Charles was already there in his tux, putting a shiny ornament on the tree, which was now lit with the multicolored lights. Beyond the window, the sidewalk was crowded with wide-eyed onlookers obviously enjoying the scene. One man, a young father with small children, had a camera and was videotaping his children by the window.

She approached Charles and tried to look calm and everydayish. The task was difficult because of the way he stared at her. His blue eyes shone and there was a certain gravity in his demeanor, as if he was dealing with some inner feeling or revelation. *Here we go again*, she thought uneasily. What made things worse for her was that he looked so handsome. The debonair black tux on his slim, athletic figure, the blond hair that picked up the window lighting, his radiant eyes—what was happening here? It was as if she were seeing him for the first time, and she liked what she saw. And she liked that he appeared to approve of what he saw. Her heart started to pound. He was her employer, her friend. Why was this whirling, off-center feeling coming over her?

"You look exquisite," he said softly as she came up to him.

"So do you," she said with a nervous little laugh.

"I've started on the ornaments," he said, not taking his eyes off her.

"So I see."

"I put up another decoration, too."

"Where?"

"Step back into the doorway you came through," he said, pointing to the doorway that was part of the display.

Surprised by the request, she did as he asked and walked back a few steps to the doorframe, then turned to face him again. She found he'd followed her.

"Look up," he said.

She did and noticed a small decoration in the middle of the top of the doorframe. It was a sprig of a plant bound with red ribbon.

"What's that?"

"Don't you know?"

Puzzled, she looked up again. "Mistletoe!"

"Right." He stepped closer. "You know what's supposed to come next."

Oh, God, she thought. He wasn't really planning on— Her heart pounded harder. "But we're in the window with everyone looking at us."

"They'd expect us to follow through with the old custom. I don't think we should disappoint them, do you?" He edged even closer.

She could feel his body heat, and she had a yen to lean into him, into the warmth. But she resisted. "I think maybe we're carrying this living display thing too far."

"I'm the store's president and the one to make that decision," he whispered, his face drawing close to hers. "I say a public kiss under the mistletoe is perfectly harmless.''

"Oh," she said, mesmerized by his voice and sky-colored eyes. She was going to argue that he'd muss her perfectly applied lipstick, but suddenly she could say no more, because he leaned in and kissed her mouth.

The kiss was brief, but potent. He slipped his arm around her back to pull her closer, kissed her intently for one full second, then let her go. She felt dazed, not sure if her feet were still on the floor.

"There." His voice was deep, breathy. "That was easy, wasn't it?"

"All in the Christmas spirit," she said, trying to make light of it though her hands were shaking. She didn't know if he'd kissed her just to entertain their audience, or if he'd put up the mistletoe on purpose to have an excuse to kiss her for the first time.

"Merry Christmas, Jenny," he said, taking her hand and squeezing it.

He'd never called her Jenny before. That and the kiss floored her. She still didn't know how seriously she should take all this, reminding herself that Charles liked practical jokes. "You've got lipstick on your mouth," she said, again keeping her tone puckish.

"Wipe it off, then."

"Do you have a handkerchief?" she asked.

"Use your fingers."

She felt a trifle shocked. Nevertheless, she raised her hand to his mouth and wiped off the traces of red with her thumb and fingertips. As she did so, his eyes took on a sensual glaze. She felt like fainting.

Rubbing her hands together to get rid of the lipstick, she said, "Let's put some ornaments on the tree, okay?" Her voice sounded out of breath.

FREE BOOKS!

FREE GIFT!

PLAY THE "LUCKY 7" SLOT MACHINE GAME!

AND YOU CAN GET
FREE BOOKS PLUS
A FREE GIFT!

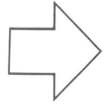

NO COST! NO OBLIGATION TO BUY!
NO PURCHASE NECESSARY!

PLAY "LUCKY 7"
AND GET FIVE FREE GIFTS!

HOW TO PLAY:

1. With a coin, carefully scratch off the silver box at the right. Then check the claim chart to see what we have for you—FREE BOOKS and a gift—ALL YOURS! ALL FREE!

2. Send back this card and you'll receive brand-new Silhouette Yours Truly™ novels. These books have a cover price of $3.50 each, but they are yours to keep absolutely free.

3. There's no catch. You're under no obligation to buy anything. We charge nothing—ZERO—for your first shipment. And you don't have to make any minimum number of purchases—not even one!

4. The fact is thousands of readers enjoy receiving books by mail from the Silhouette Reader Service™ months before they're available in stores. They like the convenience of home delivery and they love our discount prices!

5. We hope that after receiving your free books you'll want to remain a subscriber. But the choice is yours—to continue or cancel, anytime at all! So why not take us up on our invitation, with no risk of any kind. You'll be glad you did!

NOT ACTUAL SIZE

This beautiful porcelain box is topped with a lovely bouquet of porcelain flowers, perfect for holding rings, pins or other precious trinkets — and is yours absolutely free when you accept our no risk offer!

PLAY "LUCKY 7"

**Just scratch off the silver box with a coin.
Then check below to see the gifts you get.**

YES! I have scratched off the silver box. Please send me all the gifts for which I qualify. I understand I am under no obligation to purchase any books, as explained on the back and on the opposite page.

201 CIS AWPS
(U-SIL-YRT-02/96)

NAME

ADDRESS   APT.

CITY   STATE   ZIP

 WORTH FOUR FREE BOOKS PLUS A FREE PORCELAIN TRINKET BOX

 WORTH THREE FREE BOOKS

 WORTH TWO FREE BOOKS

🔔🔔🍒 **WORTH ONE FREE BOOK**

THE SILHOUETTE READER SERVICE™: HERE'S HOW IT WORKS

Accepting free books places you under no obligation to buy anything. You may keep the books and gift and return the shipping statement marked "cancel". If you do not cancel, about a month later we'll send you 4 additional novels, and bill you just $2.69 each plus 25¢ delivery and applicable sales tax, if any.* That's the complete price, and—compared to cover prices of $3.50 each—quite a bargain! You may cancel at any time, but if you choose to continue, every other month we'll send you 4 more books, which you may either purchase at the discount price...or return at our expense and cancel your subscription.

*Terms and prices subject to change without notice. Sales tax applicable in N.Y.

He smiled as if reading her reaction. "Ornaments, mistletoe and you. This is going to be a great Christmas! I'd like to live in this window with you for a long time."

Mind blown, she stepped around him and picked up an ornament. "People would get pretty bored watching us," she said, still trying for a light touch.

Charles followed suit and found a candy cane, which he hung on a branch. "I don't think so. We've moved from a G rating to PG. Maybe we'll go on to R."

Knowing he had to be kidding, she opened her eyes wide in mock humor. "We have? With a kiss? What's next that'll make us R-rated?"

His eyes gleamed. "Anything you want."

"Okay," she said, finding her stride in the chaos of her mind. "I'll smear whipped cream on your nose and lick it off!"

He looked at her for a moment, then broke into laughter. "I'm game. Anytime!"

That night in her apartment, Jennifer sat on her couch and watched the end of the late-evening news with the volume turned down. She was trying to think through what had happened that afternoon. After the whipped-cream joke, Charles's behavior went back to normal, more or less. But in the evening, in the bedroom display, he'd obviously ogled her instead of being surreptitious about it as he had in the past. At 10:00 p.m., as they'd left the window, he'd put his arm around her. He did it in a friendly sort of way, but even so, he'd never done that before, except for the night when he was trying to make Delphine jealous.

Jennifer didn't know what to make of it all. Charles looked and behaved very much as if he was attracted to her, but she still couldn't quite believe it. And she didn't know how to respond to it.

She was startled by the phone ringing on the end table next to her.

"Jennifer? It's me, Charles."

"Charles?" she repeated, astonished. He'd never phoned her before.

"Turn on your TV to the news." He told her what channel.

"I've got it on," she said.

"You do? Then you heard that they're going to show a tape of us."

"What! I had the volume down. What tape?"

"I don't know. They just said that after the commercial they'd show 'a daring kiss at Derring Brothers caught on tape.'"

Jennifer grabbed her remote and turned up the volume. The commercial had just ended. The slick male newscaster talked about the Derring Brothers' Christmas promotion and said, "The living display really came alive late this afternoon. A man who had brought along his camcorder to film his kids enjoying the holiday department-store displays caught the action. As you probably know, Derring Brothers' new president, Charles Derring, is spending twelve hours a day living in the store's windows with Jennifer Westgate, a store employee. As they decorated a Christmas tree, sparks started to fly. Take a look at this...."

Oh, no, Jennifer thought.

"Are you watching?" Charles asked.

She'd almost forgotten she still had the phone at her ear. "Yes!" She could see herself on the screen now, standing in the doorway as Charles approached her. The amateur photographer couldn't have shot them at a better angle. As

Charles kissed her and drew her against him, Jennifer was shocked at how passionate it looked. "Oh, God, this is so embarrassing," she murmured.

"Embarrassing?" Charles said. "I think it's great!"

"How about that?" the newscaster said with a grin when the clip ended. "We'll try to get an update on this apparent department-store romance for tomorrow's newscast. Stay tuned and keep that mistletoe handy! Good night."

Jennifer turned off the TV. "What's great about it?" she asked Charles, feeling mortified.

"It's terrific free publicity for Derring Brothers," he said. "And . . . you looked beautiful on TV. We've followed through with this assignment better than anyone had a right to hope, considering neither of us wanted to do it. I'm proud of you!"

"But all of Chicago has seen us kissing! They're making a big romance out of it."

"So?"

"So—it's not true. I mean, we're just friends."

There was silence for a moment. "Yeah, just friends." His voice sounded a bit flat now. "Well, a romance, real or imagined, always draws interest. The public was primed to look for a romance because of the questions at the press conference. In fact, things have happened just as you predicted. Try to be happy about it."

She thought he sounded disappointed and considered the possible reason why. "You didn't mean that kiss for real, did you? It was just for fun. Wasn't it?"

There was silence on the line again, then, "Did you think it was fun?"

"Well . . . sure. But you meant it to entertain the sidewalk crowd, right?"

"I meant it for our entertainment, as well."

"You did?"

"Yes."

"And . . ." She swallowed. "Were you entertained?"

"Yes!"

"Oh. So, are you going to have a kiss written into our daily sheet of directions?" she asked, trying for humor since she didn't know how else to handle the conversation.

"Sounds good to me," he replied, warmth returning to his voice. "Would you like that?"

Jennifer's heartbeat was going haywire. "Well, sure. Anything for Derring Brothers. Maybe we ought to draw the line at the whipped-cream thing, though. I don't think it would be good for the store's image to go all the way to an R rating."

He laughed. "We'll hold the whipped cream for now. Thanks for . . . cooperating. On the kiss, I mean."

"That's okay."

There was a silence again, as if he was looking for something else to say or waiting for her to say something.

"I'd better go to bed and get my beauty sleep," she told him, "so I'll look good for the window tomorrow."

"I guess so," he said, his voice sounding wistful. "I'll see you tomorrow, then."

"Good night."

"Night."

She got ready for bed and turned out the lights to go to sleep. But she couldn't. What would a millionaire's son, probably already a millionaire himself, see in her? It was only the makeup and hairstyling that made her beautiful enough to attract a man who could have his pick. What would happen when the week was over, and she went back to looking like her old self? His interest would certainly wane. It was the artificial glamour he was attracted to.

He'd never made a pass at her in Housewares, when she wore her business suits and a simple hairstyle.

This "romance," if it was one, would be fleeting, she was sure. But it would be interesting to go along with it while it lasted. She was finding that Charles looked more appealing to her with every hour they passed together in the window. Maybe it was only because she was on the rebound from Peter. But since a romance with Charles couldn't possibly last anyway, what was the harm? Having Charles's attentions, even for a while, would lift her spirits. She should loosen up and look at it as fun, as Charles apparently was. A window-display fling. How many women could claim that in the history of their love life?

As she drifted off to sleep, Jennifer made a decision. Why not go for it? As long as it didn't go too far. And how could it? Love that was on display in a store window couldn't display anything all that dangerous. There was no way they could ever actually get to an R rating, much less X. This would be a safe fling—the only kind Jennifer would ever allow herself to have.

6

The next morning, as she was leaving her dressing room wearing a long skirt and matching sweater, she found Jasper Derring apparently waiting for her.

"Good morning, Mr. Derring," she said to the diminutive but formidable gentleman. She'd occasionally run into him on breaks, and he always complimented her in some way. Charles had mentioned that because he was scheduled to be in the window all week, Jasper had volunteered to take over some of Charles's regular duties, so the store would continue to run smoothly during its busiest season. For this reason, Jasper had been at the store much more often than he'd been since he'd retired.

"Morning, Jennifer. You look lovely as always." He drew a bit closer and lowered his voice as some people passed by in the aisle. "I just wanted to say I'm pleased with the publicity you and Charles are drawing. The TV reports last night and the front-page photo in this morning's paper of you and him under the mistletoe are charming."

Jennifer felt herself blushing. She was surprised Jasper approved. "I'm glad you're happy about that. I found it a little embarrassing."

"Oh, it was a harmless kiss," he told her in a reassuring tone. "And you handled it in just the right way, looking sweet and demure. It adds a bit of old-style romance to Derring Brothers' Christmas promotion. Our sales were rising even before last night, and now I'm sure they'll rise even faster.''

"That's fine, but people may be disappointed afterward when they find Charles and I aren't . . . you know, aren't really involved with each other.'' She felt self-conscious about her secret new crush on Jasper's son, and took an all-business tone of voice to try to cover her wayward feelings about Charles. "If they're expecting his quip about wedding invitations to come true, I'm afraid they'll be disillusioned. I hope that doesn't hurt the store's business when Christmas is over.''

The lines in Jasper's forehead deepened and he seemed to be weighing seriously what she said. In fact, she thought he looked genuinely worried as he studied her face and delved into her eyes. His own dark eyes had the curious quality of making one feel that he could see through flesh and bone all the way into one's mind.

But in a moment, he smiled, took her hand and patted it, and said, "It's good of you to be concerned, but don't worry. If publicity mistakes are made, it's not your fault, it's ours.''

"So, if Charles kissed me for the publicity angle, and it backfires, it's his fault?'' she blurted out, obliquely fishing for another opinion on the event, since Charles's explanation of the kiss had been ambiguous.

Again, Jasper's eyes pierced hers. "I don't think it will backfire. As to why he kissed you—which I sense is what you're asking—it wasn't something he discussed with me beforehand,'' he said with humor. "But I imagine it was an impulse on his part. My son, as you must already know, is very impulsive. It's perhaps his worst—but sometimes his best—trait. When he's impulsive, he's at his most brilliant.''

Jennifer nodded and said nothing, too addlepated to think of anything more to ask or add to their conversation. She wondered why Jasper was spending so much time speaking with her.

Jasper scratched a bushy gray eyebrow. ''You didn't mind the kiss too much, did you?''

She smiled disconcertedly. ''No, I…didn't mind. It was all for entertainment. That's what Charles said.''

''Mmm.'' Jasper made the disapproving sound deep in his throat. ''That's Charles for you,'' he murmured. His demeanor quickly changed and he grew courteous again. ''I have to attend to some store matters, but I'm glad we were able to have this chat. We're all very pleased with you and hope you aren't finding being a living mannequin too onerous,'' he said with a smile.

''No, it's been more enjoyable than I expected,'' she replied politely, finding her own composure again. ''By the way, I thought I saw you outside in the crowd for a second yesterday afternoon.''

Jasper grinned broadly. ''You have a sharp eye. Yes, I've been outside looking in on you two from time to time, just to see the display as the public sees it. It's really rather fascinating. There's a voyeur aspect about it, and I think that's what attracts the crowds.'' He buttoned his suit jacket. ''Have to go. Keep up the good work, my dear!'' He walked off down the aisle between clothing racks.

A bit late now, Jennifer hurried to the kitchen display window and entered it through the small, camouflaged door.

Charles was already there, wearing a solid-colored red apron over his sweater. She found herself in a cautious mood as she began to make breakfast with him. As she dipped thick bread into the egg batter Charles had prepared, she said, "I just spoke with your father. He was happy that we made the front page this morning."

Charles looked pleased. "I know. He called me at home before I left. Good work!"

With a laugh, she said, "I didn't arrange the photo."

"No, but if you hadn't stood still for the kiss, there wouldn't have been any tape or photo. Did you notice the crowd is bigger this morning?"

"Yes, it's amazing." She looked out at the crowd of people of all ages, watching them with eager curiosity. Many smiled or waved when they saw her glancing at them. She waved back. "Some of them will probably stay out there all day waiting for something more to happen."

"We won't disappoint them," he said, unwrapping a stick of butter.

"Oh?" She took an impish tone. "Is there a kiss written into our schedule today?"

"No," he replied. "That's up to our discretion."

The comment made her laugh ruefully. "I don't think we have much of that."

He put down the butter and edged closer. "Maybe I don't, but you always had plenty. Are you saying you've lost it?"

His shoulder touched hers and her breathing became a little faster. "What do you think?"

"I think we may have put a chink in it," he said. "I'm a bad influence on you. You used to be so proper."

"You used to say I was too proper," she reminded him. "And then you said I was changing too fast."

"You're hard to keep up with," he agreed, his voice strangely soft. "But I like the challenge."

She took a long breath and exhaled to steady herself a bit. "Will you be straight with me about something?"

"Sure. What?"

"What's going on between us?"

His blue eyes grew more intense. "I'm not sure," he said seriously. "I'm a little baffled myself. I used to think of you as the friend I liked to spar with. Now..." He looked down.

"What?"

His eyes rose to hers again. "Now I can't stop thinking about you. When I'm near you, all I want to do is touch you...kiss you."

Jennifer kept herself steady. "It's only because the makeup and hairstyles they give me make me look more like the women you're usually attracted to."

She watched his eyes move slowly over every feature of her face. "Maybe. I think all it does is make me take notice of what was there already."

"But you never wanted to kiss me before."

"Maybe I was blind."

She grew discomfited at the sweet things he was saying and looked away, wondering whether to believe him. Maybe he was just wooing her in the window for the benefit of the crowd outside. When she glanced up, he was still staring at her, his eyes shining with that same liquid quality she'd seen when he'd approached her under the mistletoe.

He took the bread out of her hands and swept her into his arms. She didn't resist, remembering her decision last night to enjoy the "romance" even if it only lasted through the end of the week. She rose up on her toes as he bent his head, and they kissed, briefly but tenderly. She smiled at him as they drew away from each other, and he looked at her with eyes that seemed to glow with joy.

Jennifer was distracted then by what sounded like distant applause. She looked out the window and saw that, indeed, the crowd outside was clapping and cheering. Embarrassed again, yet enjoying the moment, she gazed at Charles. His face beamed.

"I guess we know how to draw a crowd, don't we?" she said with humor.

Lights darted playfully in his eyes. "Isn't publicity fun?"

Charles noticed the crowds had grown even thicker by late afternoon. Several people had cameras, perhaps hoping to catch something else on film to sell to the local media. And best yet, while changing into his tux, he'd heard from his staff assistant that this year's Christmas sales had reached an all-time high and were still climbing. It gave him a satisfied feeling to know he was reaching his goal of giving Derring Brothers its best year ever.

Jennifer came into the window to join him for their usual champagne and hors d'oeuvres. She was wearing the most stunning dress he'd seen on her yet—a long, purple satin gown that came up to her neck in a triangular fashion with the shoulders left bare. Her hair was pinned up and they'd loaned her diamond-stud earrings from the jewelry department. He grinned with pride when their outdoor onlookers oohed and aahed and applauded. They hadn't done that for him when he'd appeared in his tux, but Charles didn't feel slighted. He enjoyed letting Jennifer steal the show.

"You've made an impression!" he said, rising to give her the glass of champagne he'd poured for her. He picked up his own glass and raised it in a toast. "To the most beautiful woman in Chicago!" he said.

She smiled in her modest way. Other women he'd known had expected compliments, but Jennifer always seemed genuinely surprised.

They sat down together and she looked at the food tray on the table in front of the couch.

"What's this?" she asked, pointing to a small crystal bowl. "It looks like cat food."

"Goose liver pâté," he said. "Very expensive. But it probably tastes like cat food. I've never been crazy about liver."

"Have you tried it yet?" she asked.

"No, I've been working on the shrimp cocktail."

She leaned forward and carefully spread a cracker with the pâté. He watched her, noticing how graceful her hands were, the serene, feminine way in which she moved. He could look at her hour after hour and still be fascinated. That was something he couldn't say about any other woman he'd met. At first, he'd worried that she would be too much of a distraction with her glamorous new look, but now he found himself damned happy to be so distracted. He'd felt high all day today, long before he'd drunk any champagne.

"How's the pâté?" he asked.

"Actually," she said, chewing, "it's very good. Probably fattening, but good."

"You don't have to worry about that. You're as slim as a pencil—with some marvelous curves added."

She smiled. "Thank you."

They gazed at each other for a long moment. Suddenly, the sound of knocking on the window disturbed them. Charles counted at least three people outside pounding gloved knuckles on the thick pane of glass. One young fellow shouted, "Kiss!"

Jennifer looked a little stunned, but she chuckled. "This reminds me of what people do at weddings, when they tap silverware on their plates."

More people at the window joined in. Cameras were raised to eye level.

"They won't stop till we give in." Charles eyed Jennifer. "Are you game? Shall we act like a bride and groom?"

"As long as we don't start portraying the wedding night," she quipped.

The thought set his mind reeling. He leaned toward her, and she responded by edging toward him, closing the space between them on the couch. Unfortunately, their audience was so eager and near, he felt inhibited being so closely observed. Apparently, Jennifer felt the same way. Their kiss was short and chaste, but it pleased the crowd, who applauded as cameras flashed.

Jennifer's comments comparing this to a wedding were apt, he thought as he dipped another shrimp into cocktail sauce. An idea flashed into his mind. If romance was what drew crowds, then perhaps Derring Brothers should have a mock wedding in the display windows in June. The store could hire actors or choose some engaged couple from the bridal registry. Charles made a mental note to mention the idea to his staff for consideration.

He glanced at Jennifer, looking modest and lovely, spreading another cracker with pâté and managing to maintain her composure with grace while the crowd watched her every move. She really handled this window business well. He wondered if there was some way he could have *her* play the part of the bride come June. Of course, she'd do it as a model, since she wasn't engaged to marry anyone—yet.

Thank God Peter had run off with Delphine.

Jennifer paused over the pages of the book she'd been reading every night while sitting up in bed in the display window. The book was a hardcover romance novel by a well-known author, a current bestseller. Apparently, someone in the Derring Brothers bookstore had selected it. The story had held her interest so far, but now, suddenly, the romance element was heating up. The handsome Marquis de Sans Souci was intent on having his way with plucky Arianna, whom Jennifer thought must be the most lusty virgin on the planet.

She glanced over the edge of the book at Charles, who was sitting on the workout bench with a dumbbell in his hand, elbow resting on his knee, concentrating as he lifted the dumbbell to his shoulder and down again. His burgundy silk pajama top had come partly unbuttoned, revealing some light brown chest hair. His shoulders looked broad and she could see the muscle in his arm flexing through the shiny sleeve. The black-haired marquis faded from her mind for a moment. Charles's blond hair seemed so much more appealing to Jennifer right now, bright and casual as it fell forward over his forehead.

All at once, Charles looked up at her. When his eyes connected with hers, their blue took on a vibrant hue. He paused, apparently between exercise routines, and seemed to be using the opportunity to study her face. Though both were staring at each other, neither she nor he seemed self-conscious about it. His eyes slowly drifted downward over the curves her white satin nightgown's plunging neckline exposed and the matching lace cover-up failed to conceal. She found herself unconsciously breathing in, making her breasts rise under his scrutiny. She began to feel a hint of the lust that Arianna experienced in the book.

And then somehow the faces staring at them through the window brought Jennifer back to reality. She quickly lifted the novel upward to read again. In doing so, she purposely covered her cleavage from Charles's and the audience's view.

Charles began exercising again.

As she went on reading, the love scene grew more torrid. The marquis tore off Arianna's nightclothes, fondled her lush breasts, suckled her rosy nipples, giving Arianna spasms of erotic pleasure. Jennifer began to feel warm, even in her thin nightgown. When the marquis's masculine fingers slid down Arianna's taut stomach to touch her *there,* Jennifer abruptly shut the book and tossed it aside. There was no way she could read any more with Charles looking so muscular and manly in front of her and both of them being stared at by a vigilant audience.

Charles looked up when he saw her throw the book on the pillow next to her. He seemed surprised. "Did you finish it?"

"No."

"Didn't like it?"

She tried to pull the lace robe over her low-cut nightgown, but it wasn't made to stretch that far, having been designed to reveal. "I liked it too much," she muttered.

"So why have you stopped reading?"

"Eyestrain."

He gazed at her for a long moment. "Looks like I have the better assignment for this window. You sure don't strain *my* eyes."

"I thought you didn't like me dressed so showy," she reminded him.

"I've changed my mind," he said. Again, his eyes drifted to her breasts.

She'd always thought of herself as flat-chested, at least compared to some women—women like Delphine, for instance. But Charles didn't seem to mind. Jennifer smiled quietly to herself, feeling flattered. But she reminded him, "You've got the other biceps to exercise yet."

He gave her a half smile and shifted the dumbbell to his other hand. Looking down in concentration again, he began lifting the weight slowly and rhythmically. There was a definite sensuality in the way he moved, in the effort and focus he put into it. A question unexpectedly bubbled up in Jennifer's mind—she wondered if he put the same muscular, rhythmic intensity into lovemaking. And all at once, the faces in the window faded away and a fantasy took over Jennifer's mind....

Charles set the weight on the floor, gazed at her with eyes on fire with desire, and came over to the bed. His masculine hands pulled the lace robe down over her arms and pushed aside the nightgown's thin straps. He slipped his hand beneath the satin and caressed her breast, then aggressively kissed her mouth.

Jennifer's breaths came faster and soon caught in her throat as she imagined Charles kissing her neck, then hotly suckling her nipple. Her fantasy, inspired by the book, proved better than the book. Jennifer grew even more warm, light-headed and breathless. She felt almost delirious with happiness while her body became supercharged with desire.

All at once, that small part of her mind that had remained conscious of her surroundings set off an alarm bell. Everyone—the people peering through the window *and* Charles—was staring at her. She brought herself abruptly back to the here and now, banishing her delicious mental fairy tale. Breathing slowly and deeply, she tried to calm her racing pulse.

"Where were you?" Charles asked, his expression alert and curious.

She lifted her shoulders, not knowing at first how to answer. "I daydream sometimes."

"About what?" he asked.

She shrugged her shoulders again. "Magic carpet rides."

"To where?"

"Magic lands I've . . . never seen."

Charles's brows drew together, as if he didn't quite buy her answer to his question, but he went back to exercising and asked her nothing more.

Thank God, she thought, embarrassed at his questions when the answers were about him. She shouldn't be daydreaming such erotic fantasies about Charles. She may have grown attracted to him, and she wanted to go along with their brief window romance for all it was worth, but there was no use wishing for the moon.

After a moment, however, she decided that employing her imagination in such a way was probably harmless enough. Fantasies were safe, especially this one. Despite his ogling, she knew Charles, her employer, would never touch her body like that in real life. Nor could she ever respond with such abandon if he did, she reminded herself with a sigh.

Charles was glad when ten o'clock finally came. He'd had enough frustration for one day. Trying not to look at Jennifer in her pristine white nightgown that somehow still managed to give an eyeful, had been taxing enough, but then that sensual, faraway look had come over her face. He wished he knew what she'd been thinking about. He'd love to discover the secret to putting her in such a mood.

He upbraided himself for being so designing. If anything happened between them, it had to be because she wanted it to happen. He wanted it to be a mutual thing, born of equal male and female desire, not because of premeditation on his part.

Charles waved goodbye to the diehards who were still window-watching. He was surprised to see his father among them. Charles didn't know he'd had to stay so late. On Charles's last break, he had heard from his staff that a problem had developed in the store. A well-known football player who had been scheduled to sign autographs in the sports department hadn't shown up, and the many people waiting in line were justifiably upset. Charles had been rather glad to have to let his father handle the situation. He wondered how he'd managed. But Jasper looked calm and collected as he waved goodbye through the window, carrying his briefcase to go home. Charles saluted him, then turned to Jennifer.

He found her searching the bed and carpet as if she'd lost something.

"What are you looking for?" he asked.

"One of my diamond earrings is missing. It must have slipped off. The wardrobe lady and I both forgot about them when I changed, and I left still wearing them. And now one of them is gone." She pointed to her unadorned left ear. The other large diamond was still in place in her right ear.

"I'll help you look," he said, his eyes scanning the carpet.

They searched and searched, but the diamond did not turn up. Jennifer grew more and more concerned.

"What if it's lost?" she asked him. "It's a real diamond. I don't know why they let me wear them."

"Only real diamonds would catch the lights and give off the proper flash. It was my idea to use real stones for your jewelry. Don't worry, if it's lost, Derring Brothers can absorb the cost."

"But still, I shouldn't have been so careless," she fretted. "I didn't realize it was missing until a minute ago."

A half hour went by as they continued to look over every square inch of the window display. Then, as Jennifer was bending over, looking under the bed, Charles saw the earring slip out of her nightgown and roll onto the carpet. It had apparently fallen down her chest and into the inner folds of satin that covered her breasts.

Jennifer grabbed the diamond and touched the spot on her nightgown from where it had fallen. "Here it is! I felt it fall out. It was there all the time."

Lucky diamond, Charles thought. "Good. Now you won't have to lose any sleep. It's almost eleven. Let's go home!"

"I hope the wardrobe lady hasn't left yet," Jennifer said as she walked with him out the small door into the main part of the store.

The store looked absolutely empty.

"I'll check the dressing room," she said. She walked off to the room in the women's day-wear section that she'd been using to change.

Charles, meanwhile, walked around and called out, "Anybody here?"

The store lights were on, as they always were for security reasons. He checked the main doors and found them locked. He went around the perimeter of the entire first floor, checking every door. They were all locked. Jennifer came running up to him in her robe and nightgown, clutching her handbag, as he went back to the point at which he'd started.

"No one's here, Charles! Could everyone have left? Did they forget about us?"

Charles gazed around his festively decorated but empty department store. "I have a feeling they did."

"How will we get out?" she asked.

He chewed his lip, thinking. "That's a good question."

"What do you mean?"

"The security people lock all the doors and set the perimeter alarm before they leave. They can't be opened from the inside or the outside unless you have a key and know the alarm code."

Jennifer looked nervous. "Don't you have a key?"

"No."

"You don't have a key to your own store?"

"No," he told her. "Not with me. I'm never here this late, nor do I ever open up in the morning. The security people are hired to take care of that. And because of this window-duty thing, and all the changes of clothes I have to make, I left all my keys and credit cards in my safe at home, so they wouldn't get misplaced or fall into the wrong hands."

"So you're saying we can't get out?"

"No—unless I can call someone to come back and let us out," he said, thinking aloud.

Jennifer's face brightened. "Could you call the head of security?"

"Yes, or anyone in security—if I had their phone numbers. To get that, I'd have to go up to my office."

"Well, let's do that," she said eagerly.

Charles drew a long breath and rubbed his forehead. "The door to my office is locked, though. And I don't have that key with me, either."

"What about someone else's office?"

Charles thought over the suggestion. "It's worth a try. The elevators are off. I'll have to walk up."

"I'll go with you."

"You don't have to."

"I'd rather. I'm . . . kind of scared here all alone."

He took her hand. "We're not in any danger. Come on."

They walked up nine floors on the escalators, which weren't moving. The tenth floor could only be reached by a special elevator, but it was shut down, and they had to use a fire-escape stairwell Charles knew about.

They were out of breath when they reached his office door, which indeed was locked. It wasn't the day for the cleaning people to come, either. She followed as he checked his vice president's door, the financial secretary's door and his other colleagues' doors. All were locked. He walked through the outer room where the secretaries worked, trying the drawers of their desks, but everything was shut tight.

"I'm glad to know they're so good about following my orders to keep everything secure," Charles said with irony. "It doesn't look like anybody accidentally left out a listing of employees' home phone numbers."

"Don't you know any by heart?" Jennifer asked. "You must have had to call your vice president or other colleagues at home once in a while."

He chuckled. "That's the price we pay for modern technology. My phones here and at home are all state of the art. I just press a button when I want to call someone, and the phone does the dialing. I don't know anybody's number by heart. Except yours. I had to look yours up at home and dial it myself, since you're not programmed into my phone yet."

"That's a big help," she said, unamused.

"We can call the fire department or the police," Charles suggested, though he was reluctant to go to that extreme. He didn't mind staying in the store overnight, but he had to consider Jennifer. "They could get us out, I imagine."

Jennifer looked troubled. "But that could draw more publicity."

"I hadn't thought of that." Charles raised his eyebrows, realizing the potential newsworthiness of the situation if the fire department or police were called. "Maybe that's what we should do."

"Is publicity all you can think of?" she asked with a tinge of hostility. "If it gets out that you and I got stuck here in the store together after hours, everyone would assume... well, you know what they would assume! The public already thinks we've got some hot romance going because we keep kissing for them in the window. How can you even think of calling the police?"

"I'm only thinking of you," he said. "I thought you wanted to get out of here."

"I do! But I don't want everyone to think we...we..."

"I get your point," he said, wishing she didn't think the idea was so awful.

"Would it be good publicity for Derring Brothers?" she asked, as if sensing he was unconvinced. "This is supposed to be a family store. Your father built up its reputation that way. Do you think it would be good for the store's image if its new president is found in a scandalous situation with one of his female employees? We've already been on the edge of poor taste with the window display."

"We have?"

"Well, me in these flimsy nightgowns, you in your pajamas."

"But we always stay at least ten feet apart."

"It's the idea that's tantalizing enough!"

"The public seems to be enjoying it. No one seems turned off. The media haven't accused us of bad taste."

"Not yet," she said, pacing around him in her slippers. "But if they find out we've spent even an hour together alone in the store, dressed as we are, the whole thing could turn sour."

"I don't agree," he said, "but I won't argue. If you don't want to call the police to rescue us, then we won't. I don't want you embarrassed in any event."

"So what will we do?" she asked.

Charles was momentarily stumped. Suddenly, he straightened up as the obvious answer flashed into his mind. "My father! I should have thought of that before. I know his phone number—my parents still live in the house I grew up in. He ought to be home by now. I'll phone him, and he can contact some other employees who can help us out. He'll have their numbers at home, like I do."

"Thank heaven!" Jennifer said with relief.

Charles went to a desk phone and dialed. He heard two rings and then his father's recorded message came on. Disappointed, Charles summed up their predicament into the answering machine and asked his father to do what he could.

"He wasn't home?" Jennifer said when Charles hung up.

Charles checked his watch. "No. My mother may be out late visiting her sister. But Dad should be home anytime now. I saw him leaving. He'll call soon, don't worry. Are you hungry?"

"Yes," she said.

"Let's go down and raid the gourmet foods department. We can bring some snacks back up here and eat while we wait for the phone to ring."

She smiled for the first time since she'd found the diamond. "That sounds good. I should change, though."

"Then you have to go all the way back down to the first floor," he said. "You can grab your clothes from the dressing room when we're about to be rescued."

"I suppose that's more logical," she agreed with reluctance. "I should have changed when I first left the window, but I was so panicked because no one was around, I didn't even think about it. At least I remembered to grab my purse."

"Are you cold? We aren't under the window lights anymore."

"A little. I'll warm up when we get something to eat."

He nodded. "You're a trooper! Come on, let's raid the pantry."

They went down three floors and quickly surveyed the canned goods and boxed foods in the sumptuously decorated gourmet foods department, which had display cases overlaid with Portuguese tile and tableaux of country picnics painted on the walls. Charles had commissioned the refurbishment and was very pleased with the way it had turned out.

"It's okay to take anything here?" Jennifer asked.

"Anything you want. It's on me," he said.

She picked up a Gouda cheese, some water crackers and a can of stuffed grape leaves imported from Greece. "Where's the goose liver pâté we were eating before?" she asked.

He took a container from a refrigerated case across the aisle and handed it to her. Then he picked up a can opener and a couple of plastic knives from a box behind a counter. The knives were used when the store provided samples of spreads for customers. He found some small paper plates, too. Lastly, he went to the wine counter and chose a bottle of champagne from the refrigerated display unit.

"See anything else you want?" he asked.

"No, this will be plenty. Do we need the champagne?"

"It'll make the time go faster."

"I just hope we aren't sloshed by the time we're rescued."

"It won't be that long," Charles assured her. "In fact, we'd better get back up to the executive floor so we don't miss my father's phone call."

They hiked back upstairs carrying their food and wine. When they reached the outer office, Charles moved a couple of the secretaries' chairs together by a cleared-off desk and they opened up the containers of food. He got cups from the corner where the coffeemaker was located and poured them both some champagne.

Midnight arrived. Much of the food had been consumed and half the champagne. Charles found himself enjoying the situation. He gazed at Jennifer and thought she didn't look too unhappy. In fact, she appeared to be in a rather mellow mood. Maybe it was due to the champagne, but he was glad she was adapting well to this unforeseen circumstance.

The more he thought about it, however, the stranger it seemed that they had been forgotten, that no one had thought to check the window before closing for the night, that the wardrobe people hadn't missed them coming back to change to go home. Everyone must have been in a huge rush to leave tonight. In the morning, Charles would have the matter investigated, for more than one person must have either left early or been lax in attending to their duties.

He checked his watch again. "I wonder why my father hasn't called."

"Maybe you should try phoning him again. It's after midnight. He must be home by now."

Charles got up and walked to another desk, pressed the buttons on the phone and listened to it ring. Again, he got the recorded message.

"That's odd," he said. He pressed his lips together.

"Wouldn't someone be home at this hour?" Jennifer asked.

"You'd think so. Maybe they had the ringer turned down. They have a pedigree poodle that's high-strung, and the sound hurts its ears."

Jennifer poured herself some more champagne. "So I guess we're stuck here for the night."

"Unless you want to call the police."

She shook her head. "No way. We've been here alone for two hours. They'd wonder what we were doing all that time before we decided we wanted to be rescued."

He sat down next to her again. "What will we tell everyone when we're discovered in the morning? Won't that look even worse?"

"Don't the security people arrive first to open up?"

"Yes."

"Do you trust them?"

"Yes."

"Well then, can't you just quietly explain how we got stuck here and why we didn't want to call the police? Tell them we slept on separate floors. Swear them to secrecy."

"Sounds like a cover-up to me," Charles said with a chuckle. "Didn't Watergate teach us that a cover-up creates a worse scandal than the original misdeed?"

Jennifer looked very troubled and sipped her champagne. "I don't know what to do. We haven't done anything improper, but that's how it will look."

Charles scratched the side of his nose. "Let's see, there must be some way..." In a moment, new ideas began to flow. "Look, it's a big store, right? I can be out in the open when the security people arrive in the morning, and I'll just say that I got locked in here by accident. It'll be obvious, because I'll be unshaven. But you can just select something new off our clothing racks and put it on, then hide out somewhere in the store—in the ladies' room or maybe in the Brasserie, since the restaurants don't open until eleven and no one will be there at opening time. Then, when the store is beginning to fill with people, you can show up for window duty as if you'd just come from home. Who would have to know you were here all night?''

Jennifer chewed on her fingernail, thinking over the suggestion intently. Finally, she nodded. "I guess that might work. Okay," she said with a sigh, looking relieved. Then she glanced at him. "So what will we do—all night?''

"Sleep?" He thought again. "Not together, just...find somewhere to sleep...separately. We can go to the furniture department, or to Bedding and Linens. There are beds on display, with new mattresses, too.''

"Okay." She rubbed her eyes as if she was tired, then looked at the makeup smudges on her hands. "I need to get this makeup off first. Is there a...?" She looked around.

"The executive ladies' room is in the corner over there.''

Jennifer got up and went through the door marked Women. While she was gone, Charles eyed the open jar of pâté she'd been spreading on crackers and eating. She seemed to like the stuff. He took the plastic knife and spread a couple of the large, round crackers for himself.

Not bad, he thought. *For liver.* He'd eaten those and was spreading a few more crackers when she came out, looking more like her old self. Her face was devoid of cosmetics and she'd combed out her elaborate hairdo. It was odd seeing her freshly washed, girl-next-door face above the provocative nightgown she wore. He'd made a habit of mentally separating the Jennifer he used to know from the glamorized Jennifer he'd been sharing a window with.

But now, the two images were combined in one. And suddenly, he saw her as an entirely new person, someone he was instantly at home and comfortable with—but damned sexy, too. He looked at her in awe for a few long moments.

"Not the same without the makeup, huh?" she said, looking self-conscious under his stare.

"No," he said, finding his voice. "Better."

Her eyes widened. "Better?"

"If I kissed you now, I wouldn't get lipstick all over me."

She smiled. "I suppose that's a plus. But I'm sure you wouldn't ... want ..." She didn't finish the sentence, having apparently blurted out something she hadn't meant to say.

He put down the cracker he'd been holding and rose from his seat. Without a word, he took her in his arms and kissed her on the mouth, gently, not wanting to startle her by being too forceful.

She gave in to the kiss readily, and her willing response made his head swim. He could feel her warm body beneath the thin lace and satin. Sliding his hands to her slim waist, he pulled her closer until her stomach came against his. Bringing his hand upward over her back, he pressed her to him, feeling her soft breasts on his chest.

She raised her arms to his shoulders and circled his neck, clinging to him now. Squeezing her more tightly, he kissed her aggressively, bending her head back as he leaned over her. This was what he'd been wanting to do all evening while looking at her but not being able to touch her when they were in the window. And the reality of kissing her in private the way he wanted to was better than he'd even imagined. Desire wound its heated way through his body, and the most male part of his anatomy responded, indeed, grew demanding.

She must have felt the change in him, for all at once she broke the kiss and stepped backward. Her face showed alarm, but he could also see the glimmer of sensuality in her eyes. It was the same glaze of desire he'd seen cross her face earlier in the window, when she'd said she was daydreaming.

"Charles," she gasped, breathless and disconcerted. "We shouldn't kiss like this."

"Why not?"

"We're all alone here."

Her logic escaped him. "All the more reason to kiss the way we really want to, with no audience watching our every move."

"But it could lead to..." She swallowed. "We might get carried away."

"Is that so bad?"

She looked at him as if he were crazy. "Charles, you own the store and I'm your employee."

He wished she didn't always remind him of that. "I know. But if we have a deep attraction for each other, why should we let circumstances get in our way? It's not as if one of us is married, or even dating anyone else. Since my ex and your ex ran off with each other, we're both unattached."

"But, Charles, you should consider the circumstances—the problems with getting involved with someone who works for you."

He took her in his arms again. "I think we should just forget our work status and be plain old Jenny and Charley, doing what their hearts tell them to do."

"And what's that?" she asked in a shocked whisper.

"Get to know each other better," he said, kissing her jaw, then her neck.

"Charles," she said, pushing against his chest, "I think we should act responsibly."

He studied her for a moment, amused and disappointed. "What about all your talk of breaking loose from your mold? You said you wished you could experience a grand passion, like Peter and Delphine."

Her eyes widened as she stared at him, her lips slightly parted. His words seemed to be sinking into her mind in some profound way. She blinked and looked down. "I know I said that. But... that was just talk." She glanced up with a feeble smile. "I could never really be like that, give in to p-passion that way."

"It might do you good to try to let go," he said softly.

"No." She shook her head for emphasis, drawing away from him again. "I'm sure I'd regret it later. Who knows what the consequences would be if we...?" She stared at him. "What exactly are we talking about? Are you saying you'd like to...?"

"Make love with you," he said when she couldn't seem to voice the words.

"You really want to? With me?"

"It's all I've been able to think about every evening, looking at you in one sexy nightgown after another. I didn't foresee that this would happen, but since it has... I... I realized that I wanted more from the woman I've been trying all week not to lust after. That's you."

She sadly shook her head. "But, Charles, it's all artificial. You didn't feel any desire for me when we worked together in Housewares."

"Because I didn't realize then that I was attracted to you."

"You didn't realize it because you weren't," she insisted. "If we went through with what you're suggesting tonight, you'd be disappointed. I'm sure I'm nothing like Delphine. I can't...wouldn't know how to...to entertain you the way she did, or any of your other worldly women friends."

"You're not a virgin, though," he said, wondering how innocent she was.

"No. There was a fellow in college before I quit school," she told him, looking across the room as she spoke. "He was handsome and popular, and I was thrilled when he took me out. He wanted to go to bed, and I was inexperienced and curious about sex. But I wasn't very good at...at pleasing him, I guess. He dumped me pretty quickly."

"He was probably a love-'em-and-leave-'em type, keeping score of how many females he could seduce. Don't base the rest of your sex life on what happened with some guy on the prowl in college."

She was looking at the floor now. "Maybe you're right, but somehow I wouldn't like to test myself out again with you. I'd be too embarrassed if you were disappointed." She gazed up at him, her eyes sharp with earnestness. "How would we ever face each other afterward? How would I face myself? I'd be a salesgirl who had an affair with the store's president. It all has a tawdry, tarnished feel to it. It's not me, not how I want to conduct my life."

Charles nodded, accepting her point of view, unable to find a good argument. "I understand. I guess that's what makes you even more appealing—you have a lot of personal dignity about you." He smiled. "That's probably why they chose you for the window display, because you look respectable and classy. It's just the image we like here at Derring Brothers," he said with irony. He paused as something she said kept gnawing at him. "Can I ask you something?"

"What?"

"You said you didn't want to test yourself out with me. Were you willing to test yourself out with Peter? Or was that why you and he never slept together? You avoided the moment of truth with him, too."

"No," she said, "I was willing to sleep with him. He was the one who avoided doing it—with me anyway."

Her matter-of-factness bothered him. "So...so, why would you have made love with him, but not me? You were more attracted to him?" He was afraid to hear her answer, but needed to know.

She stared at him while she thought over her reply, wrinkling her brow as if unsure of the answer, as if having to sort it out in her mind. "No, I wasn't more attracted to him," she finally said. "I'm more attracted to you. I was even daydreaming about you tonight in the window."

"Me?" he said, his heart coming to life again. "You were daydreaming about *me?*"

"Yes. A love scene in the book I was reading got me going, but it was you I was envisioning."

"And who was I with in your daydream?"

The color in her cheeks heightened. "Me."

"You fantasized about making love with me?" He almost choked with happiness. "I've been fantasizing about you!" Stepping closer, he took her hands in his. "Why don't we fulfill our fantasies?"

"But this is real life, Charles, not a fantasy world. We'd have the real world to deal with afterward. Even if you're not disappointed with my lack of skill, you're still my employer. What would happen tomorrow?"

"Who has to know?" he said. "It can be our secret."

"Secret affairs have a way of getting out. What did you say a little while ago about cover-ups? And even if no one found out, *we* would know. We'd either have to go on with a relationship, or end it. Either way could cause problems and difficulties. And it would all end someday anyway. You'd go on to some glamorous new lady. And where would I be? It's best if we just go on as we are, as friends."

"Friends who have grown wildly attracted to each other," he said. "We can't go back to the way we used to be. And we can't stay friends this way very long."

"Why not?"

"Because I keep wanting you," he said with frustration.

"Maybe that will pass," she said. "I'm sure it will when you meet someone new, someone like Delphine who's full of glitter and fun."

"But that's the thing," he said, taking her by the shoulders. "I think I've outgrown that. I want someone stable, someone who's beautiful even without makeup—beautiful inside as well as outside. Delphine seems like kind of a bore now. You're the one who excites me."

Jennifer shook her head with disbelief. "I doubt that the feeling will last." She took his hands from her shoulders. "Let's not talk about this anymore. It's all wrong. It won't work. We'd both feel we'd made a big mistake tomorrow in the light of day."

Charles acquiesced with a quiet nod. She was right, about some aspects anyway. Simply because she was his employee, it wasn't wise of him to start an affair with her. And he couldn't predict how they would feel the morning after, though he wasn't convinced they would decide it had been a mistake. But he couldn't get over the fact that she wanted him, that the sensual look he'd seen on her face hours ago in the window had appeared because she'd been imagining herself making love with him. It just seemed unnatural not to act on their impulses.

But that was the crux of the matter. Jennifer wasn't one to do anything impulsive. And, in this knotty situation at least, she was probably right.

"We'd better figure out some sleeping arrangement, then," he told her. "You said something earlier about sleeping on separate floors. Bedding is on the third and Furniture is on the eighth. We'd be nicely separated that way."

She looked apprehensive and chewed on her thumbnail. "That would be the most appropriate thing to do, but I think I'd be afraid. The store is strangely creepy now. It's so silent and empty."

"Okay, separate beds, then. The eighth floor would be the logical choice."

"I noticed they have two beds on display now on the third floor, showing comforters and pillows and bedspreads. They always look so sumptuous when I pass by. And they're separated by the cash-register island."

"Sounds good," he said. "Let's take our food with us, what's left of it anyway. You or I may need a snack in the middle of the night if we can't sleep."

"Okay." She went to the desk where they'd eaten, threw her purse strap over her shoulder, and picked up the bottle of champagne and the paper cups they'd used. "Can you carry the crackers and pâté?"

"Sure." They'd finished off the cheese and stuffed grape leaves, and he threw away the packaging. Together, they made their way down the fire escape stairwell to the ninth floor and then down the stopped escalators to the third floor. When they arrived in the bedding section, Jennifer went straight to a twin-size bed made up with a lavender flower-print comforter and matching pillows and sat down.

She gently bounced up and down on it a few times to test it.

"It really feels comfortable. I'd like this one, if that's okay."

"Fine with me." He set down the pâté and the paper plate with the spread crackers on top of a painted wood display case in which sheets and pillowcases were stacked. "I'll pour some more champagne," he said, taking the bottle and paper cups from her. He set them on the display case and refilled each cup. "This may help us get to sleep." He handed her a cup and she took a sip. "Want any more crackers and pâté?"

"No, I'm full. You take them." She chuckled as she ran her hand over the plush comforter. "I've always thought this looked so inviting when I pass by here on break, and now I get to try it out."

He took his filled glass and sat down next to her for a moment. "I'm glad we can fulfill one fantasy for you anyway."

Her expression changed. Suddenly downcast, she gazed forlornly into her cup.

"Sorry," he said. "Didn't mean to bring that up again." He studied her and thought she looked tired and a little lost. He wondered what was going on in her mind.

"Oh, Charles," she whispered.

"What's wrong?" He turned to set his cup next to the bottle on the case in back of them, then took her hand. "I shouldn't have said that. I didn't mean to upset you."

"Am I acting like a frigid old maid?" she asked him.

"No," he assured her. "You're acting very sensibly."

She took another sip of champagne, and as she swallowed, some strong emotion seemed to come over her. She began to cry.

Charles was at a loss. "Why are you crying?"

"I never seem to get anywhere being sensible. My life is on a treadmill going nowhere."

"Jennifer," he said, squeezing her hand, "you're still in your twenties. You have lots of time to make life choices."

"Pretty soon I'll be thirty, and nothing important will have happened to me. I quit college. I never figured out what I really wanted in my life. I lost Peter. I won't have an affair with you...." she said, sniffing.

"You'll be thirty in *four years*. Aren't you only twenty-six?"

"Yes, but it's just a short hop to thirty," she said, wiping away a tear sliding down her cheek.

Charles began to suspect what might be going on. "You haven't had too much champagne, have you?"

"No. Maybe. I don't know. What difference does it make?"

"How much wine can you drink before you feel it?" he asked.

"About...half a glass."

He smiled to himself. "You've had at least twice that much." He took her cup from her and placed it next to his.

"So maybe I'm a little high," she said, a bit testy. "Who gives a damn?"

"I do. Look, I think maybe you're overtired and need some sleep. I'll go off to the other bed. But I'll be nearby, so you shouldn't be scared, okay?"

She looked at him with great sadness in her eyes. Charles didn't know what to make of it.

"Will you be all right?" he asked.

"You're leaving me, too."

This threw him. "But that was the plan. That's how you wanted it, right? Separate beds. I'll just be over there."

She nodded. "That's how I wanted it. And now you'll leave and our little romance will be all over."

"Have you changed your mind?" he asked, baffled.

"No, I'm too sensible to do that!" she replied ruefully.

"Well, then, I'll abide by your wishes." He rose from the bed. "Good night. Sleep tight," he said, leaning toward her. He kissed her on the forehead.

A tear streamed down her cheek. "I've talked you out of even trying to sweep me off my feet," she said with a forlorn sniff. "Haven't I? I'm so damned sensible, nothing exciting will ever happen in my life, because I won't let it. I live on fantasies, and even those are few and far between."

Charles was beginning to see what she really wanted. She wanted some help in overcoming her prudent inhibitions. That he could do. But should he? She was slightly inebriated, yet she was talking from the heart. Should they pass up this opportunity, an opportunity that might never come again? Or should he be sensible on her behalf, since she might be too emotional to think straight right now?

He swallowed hard. Someone ought to be sensible here. But he didn't think he could manage it. He wanted to give her what she seemed to long for, and he longed to alleviate his own frustrated desire for her. No, he decided. If she really wanted to be swept away in a grand passion, then he wanted to be the guy who did the sweeping. Charles was more than ready for a grand passion, too!

As she sat, softly crying and wiping her tears, his mind suddenly changed gears. His own fatigue from the long day disappeared in a moment and he grew more alert. Something made him look up, and all at once he became wary. There was a small, unobtrusive security camera attached to the ceiling near a pillar, seemingly focused directly on the bed, though he knew the camera had a wide-angle lens. The store had them all over, so that almost every corner was under surveillance night and day. Why hadn't he thought of that? His assurance that no one would know she'd been there all night was obviously not based on fact. What could he tell her? He'd forgotten about his own new security system? The cameras were so low key and ubiquitous that everyone, except the Security employees, forgot about them. He'd have to break the news that they'd both been recorded walking through the store together after everyone else had left. Now was definitely not the time.

But he had to figure out some way to disable this particular camera staring down at him. While Jennifer shed more tears and hid her face in her pillow, Charles noticed the large round crackers spread with pâté. Carefully, silently, he picked one up. Aiming, concentrating, he threw the cracker, pâté side up, at the camera lens.

Bull's-eye! He hit it exactly on target. It was amazing how his aim improved when the possible reward was so appealing. He stared at the cracker for a moment, afraid the pâté might not be sticky enough to hold, but the cracker stuck like glue. He exhaled an eager sigh.

Moving slowly, thinking through his approach, he sat down again next to Jennifer and set his hand on her shoulder. "You haven't entirely dissuaded me, Jenny. I'd love to make that fantasy of yours come true. All you have to do is give in and let my desire meld with yours. Fantasy fulfillment is easy. Caution is difficult. Take the easy way for a change."

She looked up from the pillow, and he gently turned her onto her back, pressing her into the comforter. He wiped away her tears with his fingers as she looked at him in glazed shock. Before she could say anything, he leaned forward to kiss her.

She responded with warm, eager lips. Her arms wound around his neck in a caressing way that made him close his eyes with indescribable longing.

But all at once, she used her hands to push him away. "Oh, Charles," she said, sounding meek. "We shouldn't."

"I think we should."

"But what about tomorrow?"

Charles slid his hand gently beneath the lace and satin that covered her small, soft breast. "We'll worry about tomorrow tomorrow." Her flesh felt warm and yielding. The taut nub of her nipple attracted his fingertips.

She gasped and closed her eyes. "Charles, Charles," she murmured with yearning.

"Do you like that?" he whispered, then kissed her mouth.

When the tender, sensual kiss was over, she opened her beautiful green eyes and in a breathless rush said, "I like it! Give me more...."

7

Jennifer swallowed as she looked into Charles's blue eyes, realizing she'd just said, "Give me more." However much her body ached for his touch, some part of her brain was suddenly alarmed, telling her she shouldn't have said that. But before she could put any further thought or words together, Charles stroked her breast again and her mind grew hazy with pleasure.

He kissed her hotly and she responded with equal ardor. In the next feverish moments, she felt his large warm hands pushing her robe and nightgown down her shoulders. Cool air on her breasts told her she was naked, but she didn't care. His mouth eagerly left hers, traveled down her neck and found her nipple, just as she had fantasized. An ecstatic whimper left her throat at the sensations he aroused.

"You're so beautiful," he murmured, caressing her. He seemed transfixed, watching her swelling mound of flesh shift as he pressed it upward. "So sexy!"

"You really think so?"

He grinned and rubbed her nose with his. "Yes, I really think so!" Then his mouth fastened on hers again. As they kissed more and more heatedly, she tried to undo the buttons of his pajama top. But her fingers were too shaky, so she ripped it open. As if spurred on by her dramatic method of ridding him of his clothing, he moved over her, sinking down on top of her, his bared chest powerful and heavy on her breasts. She could feel his chest hair on her nipples. Sliding her arms over his back, she stroked his skin. Her fingers dug under the elastic of his waistband and she found the smooth, hard mounds of his buttocks.

"That feels so good," he whispered, his breath burning her cheek. "Where did you learn that?"

"In the book," she said. She smiled and bit his earlobe. "But I always thought you had nice buns."

She could feel his body shake as he laughed. "I never thought I'd hear you say something like that. But I'm darn glad to hear it!" He shifted and she could feel his hardness against her thigh exciting her and yet giving her renewed anxiety. They kissed again, their bodies writhing together in torrid pleasure. "Jenny, I need you now...."

She knew that, but his words shook her. She took a long, quavery breath. Wanting him desperately, but afraid of disappointing him, she tried to steel herself and be daring for once in her life.

But suddenly, he stopped midkiss and looked at her. "We don't have any protection." His voice sounded ragged and breathless. "Do you want to risk it? I'm willing, but—"

"It's okay," she said, glad she remembered. "I have a couple of condoms in my purse."

He drew back, his eyes wide with incredulity. "You do?"

"Well..." She swallowed, hoping her explanation wasn't going to ruin the moment. "When I was dating Peter, I started carrying them with me, just in case he ever... But he never did, and they're still there."

"I'm damn glad he never did." Charles murmured, much amused. "For *two* reasons." His expression grew less amused and more impatient. "Better get them out."

He helped her reach for her purse. She hurriedly fished through its contents and found what she was looking for buried at the bottom.

Charles took one of the small packets from her and ripped it open. He unfastened his waistband. She saw he wore blue Jockey shorts underneath—because he'd been on display in the window, no doubt. She was glad to see he had some sense of modesty. Though when she saw him apply the protective sheath after he'd removed his clothing, she realized he had no reason to be modest. Her breathing grew thin and shallow with anticipation.

Finished, he turned to her and noticed her expression. "You're not getting cold feet, are you?"

"No!" she replied, sounding a bit brazen to her own ears. "My feet are warm, my hands are trembling, and my heart's skipping beats. But other than that, I'm just f-fine."

His eyes took on a heated, incandescent light so mesmerizing she stopped breathing altogether for a moment. His hand slid to her waist, where her nightgown had bunched. "I'm going to take this off, all right?"

She nodded, unable to speak. He pulled the white satin gown and the white satin panties he found beneath down her thighs and off her body. Tossing them aside, he moved over her again, stroking her thighs and flat stomach. His fingers slid downward toward her secret place, already slick and pulsing with her arousal. When he touched her, she cried out with acute, almost painful, pleasure. Her body convulsed slightly, her hips rising up, aching for more.

Acting on her erotic response, he slid his naked body over hers, head-to-head and toe-to-toe. She eagerly absorbed his weight upon her and instinctively wound her limbs around him. They kissed, tenderly at first and still out of breath, but soon their kisses grew more aggressive and electric. Her thighs were already parted, and her body pulsated with need. She squirmed against him, all but begging for fulfillment. And then she sharply gasped in awe as his thick member entered her. He felt almost too big for her. She closed her eyes, feeling slight pain, as if she were a virgin again. But soon the pain disappeared, and she knew only the joy of being filled.

He began firm back-and-forth movements, and she held on tightly, delirious with the sensations he drew from her body. Her hands slid to his buttocks, urging him on. She'd never dreamed lovemaking could be this exciting, this pleasure laden. She'd never imagined herself behaving this wantonly with a man. And judging by his labored breathing and low moans, she knew she was giving Charles as much pleasure as he was giving her.

As she felt her lower stomach tightening, her body edging toward release, she arched her neck and brought her legs up over his back. His pelvis ground against hers and she began to gasp loudly with each forward thrust he made.

All at once, there was a blissful, tenuous moment of suspension, and then she felt as if she were falling and falling. Her body convulsed in voluptuous spasms as searing release overwhelmed her. He squeezed her tightly as he made one final huge thrust. She felt him pulsate inside her. Moaning with satisfied exhaustion, he collapsed on her.

They lay together, limbs still intertwined, for a long moment. Jennifer had never felt so fulfilled and happy in her life. What a thrill to finally, finally, experience profound ecstasy! She felt free, truly free, for the first time. Her inhibitions were vanquished at last. Her life would never be the same, now that she knew what she'd been lacking. She prayed the overwhelming passion she'd discovered with Charles would last longer than this one unexpected, sublime night.

Charles rose up on his elbows and gazed down at her. His eyes had a glaze of satiation. "If I had ever guessed that you were such a good lover, I would have pursued you months and months ago." He moved off her to lie close to her on his side, looking down at her with amazement. "What I've been missing...." He ran his fingertips over her lips, then her breasts. "You're so sexy. So responsive." He smiled at her. "I'm going to want a steady diet of this."

She grinned, *feeling* sexy—and awed. "If I'd known how wonderful you are, I wouldn't have thought twice. You're so strong, so tender. It felt so comfortable, almost like we'd done this before."

He chuckled. "We did—in our heads, fantasizing about each other. This is a lot better."

She stroked his chest. "I know. You've convinced me." She leaned toward him to kiss him. "You've released me," she whispered. "Made me a real woman. I didn't know I could react that way, let go that way, with such abandon." Her fingers slid softly down his shoulder to his nipple and she fondled it gently as he had done to her. "You taught me things I didn't know. I...owe you...." she said, feeling surprisingly wanton again.

"Now you're a tease," he said, caressing her breast. "I like that." He kissed her, and as he did, she felt his member harden against her thigh. "What did you say about owing me?" he murmured.

She found the remaining condom and slipped it beneath his hand caressing her breast. "I have one more of these left," she said in a whispery voice. "Will that pay my debt of gratitude?"

"You're getting more provocative by the minute," he said. "Is this the real you, the you you've been hiding all this time?"

"I guess so," she replied. "I'm just getting acquainted with the real me, too."

As he ripped open the new condom, she said, "Aren't there different positions and things? Could we experiment?"

He stopped mid-rip, his eyes growing more and more blue as he stared at her. "Sure, we have all night." He eyed her with new respect. "When you turn over a new leaf, you mean business, don't you?"

"Out with the old me, in with the new," she said, chuckling at her own audacity. "I want to explore this new thing we've discovered between us. I want to know all I can about us. How much can we shock ourselves?"

"What a question!" He lay back, smiling, and pulled her toward him. "I think you should be on top this time."

She gasped at what seemed like a daring idea, but soon she found herself happily astride him, the length of him deliciously inside her, as she moved up and down over him. He seemed to enjoy the bouncing of her breasts, and his hands rose up to caress her.

They played and teased until they writhed in joyous, satiating bliss once again. Afterward, they lay in each other's arms, all passions momentarily spent, and fell asleep.

Hours later, Jennifer awoke abruptly and found herself naked in Charles's arms on a bed in the empty department store. Instantly, she remembered. She looked at Charles, still asleep near her shoulder. His blond hair was mussed and his eyes were closed. She gazed over his manly body and remembered their intimacy, the fulfillment he'd given her. They'd made love in a haze of champagne and unexpected circumstances. Now that morning had come, would everything be different? How would he feel about her when he woke up in a few minutes and found himself in bed with her?

A pang of anxiety wound through her stomach, making her realize something she'd been pushing out of her mind. She loved Charles. She wasn't sure how long she'd been in love with him; perhaps her feelings even dated back to the time when they worked together in Housewares. But he seemed so different from her, in personality and in social status, that she'd thought him unattainable. So she pretended, and even had convinced herself, that nothing other than a working friendship could ever happen between them. She told herself she wouldn't want him even if he were interested in her. That way she could feel that she was rejecting him before he could ever have a chance to reject her.

They *were* different. How could they ever wind up together in a permanent relationship? This window-display "fling" she'd allowed herself to have with him had gotten way out of hand, but it was all she'd probably ever have— and it was worth it.

All at once, Charles opened his eyes. Jennifer braced herself, fearing she'd see shock and dismay on his face at waking to find himself naked with her. But instead, she saw only a sleepy, adoring glow in his blue eyes.

"Is it morning?" he asked.

"I think so. My watch says six-thirty."

He glanced at his watch. "Well, at least we woke up before the security people arrive." He gazed at her. "How do you feel?"

"Okay. Not enough sleep, but I'll get by."

"You look wonderful. Lack of sleep suits you. Or maybe it's what kept us awake that suits you."

She smiled. "I'd give up sleep anytime for more of what we shared last night."

His eyes brightened. "You aren't sorry, then?"

"No. Are you?"

"No!"

"I probably ought to be ashamed, but somehow I'm not. Not the least bit."

He took her hand. "Good. I don't want you to have any regrets." He glanced at the rumpled bed and their clothes strewn around. "We have to figure out what to tell people, though, when they discover we've been locked in here all night."

Jennifer drew her brows together. "But you figured that out last night. I'll borrow some outfit from the store and hide and—"

He appeared hesitant and shook his head. "No, I realized that plan won't work. I forgot that there are hidden security cameras around the store. They might have caught us walking through the store together, so I don't think we can pretend you weren't here. You may be on tape."

A wave of panic shot through Jennifer. She'd heard about the store's new surveillance cameras, though she didn't know where they were. Why hadn't she thought of that herself? How could they both have forgotten?

"Oh, my God!" she exclaimed as she frantically sat up and looked around her. "There aren't any cameras here, are there? We didn't get taped making love, did we?"

He sat up, cupped a hand on either side of her head, and made her look at him. "Jennifer, believe me, what happened last night didn't get taped. But we may have to go back to your plan of telling the head of security what happened and asking him to keep it quiet. I'll . . . ask him to destroy all the tapes from last night, so there's no evidence you were here. Meanwhile, pick out an outfit, lie low, and then show up as if you were reporting to work as usual. We'll use both plans."

"How do you know we didn't get taped in bed?" she asked.

He took her by the shoulders and gave her a playful little shake. "I'm the president of the store, am I not? Wouldn't I know where the cameras are and what they're taping?"

"You forgot that your store even had cameras," she reminded him.

"I know. It was stupid of me. The champagne and being near you made my mind fuzzy. But I'm satisfied and sober now, and I know what I'm talking about. So don't worry. Okay?"

"Okay," she said. But inside, she still felt uneasy.

She picked out a blue suit from the career women's clothing section that was in keeping with her normal manner of dressing for work, grabbed some new underwear and panty hose, and took them upstairs to the executive women's room she'd used earlier. She was willing to go all the way back up to the top floor because that ladies' room, she'd noticed, had a shower—perhaps for women executives who used their lunch hour to work out. She showered, blew her hair dry, put on the new garments, and went all the way down to the first floor. There she got the suit she'd worn to work yesterday, bundled it up in a Derring Brothers shopping bag, and left it in the dressing room to take home later. Then she went up to the Brasserie, which, as Charles had predicted, was perfectly empty, and waited.

Just before opening time, when store employees were arriving, she went back down to the first-floor dressing room. Mr. James and Christine greeted her as they had every other day. As she sat down to have her hair and makeup done, she felt confident that no one suspected what had happened during the night. It was Jennifer's beautiful secret.

Christine gave her a simple pageboy hairstyle that morning, and Mr. James was getting more efficient every day at her makeup, so Jennifer found herself ready early. She decided to look for Charles and see if she could speak to him privately, to ask how he'd handled the security department and if he'd gotten them to keep quiet and destroy the tapes. One of his assistants said he'd gone up to the executive floor, so Jennifer headed upstairs again, using the elevators. There, she found Charles's office door open. She peeked in and saw him talking to Herb Anderson, the middle-aged, red-haired man who was head of the store's security. Herb had probably let Charles into his own office, since Charles had left his keys at home.

She paused outside, hesitant to be a disruption while Charles was still speaking with Herb. Herb was laughing, however, and Jennifer grew alarmed at the taint of his laughter. It sounded like that raunchy, between-us-boys sort of amusement that had always raised Jennifer's hackles. Obviously, Herb was enjoying the fact that the store's president had had a little overnight hanky-panky. Then she saw Herb hand Charles a videocassette.

"Found the one you wanted," he told Charles. "You'll see for yourself when you play it."

"Thanks," Charles said as he took the tape. "Now, you'll keep this to yourself?"

"You bet, Mr. Derring. You can count on me. Wouldn't want you or the elder Mr. Derring in the soup. Got too much respect for you both. Good thing I arrived early this morning, eh? Before anyone else in security could check the tapes."

"Right!" Charles agreed. "Thanks, Herb. You'll get a little something extra this Christmas."

"That's very kind of you."

"You're a loyal employee! I'll let you go—I have a phone call to make."

As Herb saluted him and left without noticing her, Charles picked up the phone and dialed before Jennifer could even enter the room. Again, she hung back and waited, falling into the respectful pattern of an employee with her employer. Had she already forgotten she'd slept with him last night?

"It's Charles Derring. Look, I need to talk to you during my break from window duty this morning. I've got a hot new idea for publicity, and I want you guys to get on it. If we handle it right, this one may even get us on 'Stop the Press' or one of those other TV shows. Can you see me? Great. Gotta go."

As Charles hung up, Jennifer was wondering what the new publicity idea was and what it might have to do with the tape. What was on the tape? she wondered. Charles had assured her that there was no camera near the bed where they'd made love. She thought of the popular TV show he'd mentioned, "Stop the Press." It was one of those tabloid news shows that sometimes reported genuine news and sometimes dug up whatever they could that was shocking. Sometimes they even aired amateur videotapes that had caught something risqué with black patches covering strategic spots to make it "okay" to show on TV.

Jennifer got a sick feeling in her stomach. Instead of going into Charles's office, she quietly slipped away and rushed down the fire-escape stairs, where no one would see her, to the next floor. There, she took an elevator down to the third floor. She hurried to the bedding and linens area. When she reached the bed, whose comforter and pillows she herself had fluffed and straightened, she looked around for a security camera. A maintenance man on a ladder drew her attention, and she looked up. She felt the blood drain from her face as she saw what he apparently was cleaning with a cloth—a small, square video camera! Charles had lied when he'd told her there was no camera taping them, she realized with a feeling of nausea. They *had* been taped! And she was willing to bet the tape Herb handed Charles had been that very one.

And now, for publicity, Charles wanted to give the tape to a tabloid TV show! Or was he going to sell it? Had he gone mad? She recalled how excited he'd been when their window kiss had been caught on tape and shown on TV. Did he think a tape of him and his window-display mate mating would be even better publicity for Derring Brothers? Had he made love with her for the sole purpose of creating such a provocative tape?

Feeling faint, she sat down on the bed for a moment. She remembered all their heated passion, how naked they'd been with no covers over them. She cupped her hands over her face in horror when she remembered the position she'd assumed with him when they'd made love the second time. The camera would have caught an eyeful.

She got up and raced downstairs to the display window, where Charles would now be headed. She had to stop him before he went through with this horrible new promotion angle. And then she'd kill him for tricking her into making love, for putting her reputation up for grabs just so he could grab more publicity!

When she entered the kitchen display window, he wasn't there yet, though a crowd was already gathered outside, waiting. She returned their waves without enthusiasm. An instruction sheet had been left for them on the counter. After glancing at it, she got a carton of eggs out of the refrigerator and some cheese, tomatoes and green peppers, all supplied for the omelets they were supposed to prepare. All the while, Jennifer's temper was building. How could Charles have done this to her? How could she have trusted him? How could she have been so stupid as to make love with him?

She was taking eggs out of the carton to break into a bowl, when all at once he came through the small, concealed door and walked up to her.

"Good. One of us is on time," he said in an energetic, jaunty tone. "I got delayed with a few phone calls."

She turned on him, an egg in her hand. "You swine!"

"Huh?"

"How could you?" For emphasis, she threw the egg at him.

Skillfully, he caught it with one hand and put it back in the carton. But his face was a picture of wide-eyed shock. "What? What's wrong?"

"You told me there was no camera on us last night!"

"There wasn't," he said.

For that, she threw another raw egg at him, which he also caught.

"I went back there," she informed him. "There's a security camera pointed straight at the bed! I know, because a man was up there cleaning it!"

Charles's expression changed. "I . . . I threw a cracker spread with pâté at the lens. The lens was covered. That's why the maintenance man was cleaning it."

"Threw a cracker at it?" she said with disbelief.

"When you weren't looking. I'm a good shot."

"Then what about the tape Herb gave you this morning?" she asked. "What was on it?"

"How do you know about that?"

"I went up to see you, and Herb was in your office. I saw him give you a tape, and you swore him to secrecy. And then you got on the phone and talked about giving the tape to 'Stop the Press'!"

Charles's blue eyes squinted. He shook his head. "No, Jennifer. Let me explain—"

"Why you seduced me in front of a camera to get us on tape, so you'd have something to sell to tabloid TV? That'll take a lot of explaining! Is publicity all you can think of? How could you humiliate me this way? How could you be so duplicitous? Pretending you were attracted to me—and I was stupid enough to believe it!" She flung another egg at him.

Again, he caught it. "Jennifer, will you listen a minute? Put down that tomato!" He set the eggs he'd caught on the counter away from her, and shoved the carton out of her reach. The tomato, too. "When Herb came in, the first thing he said was that my father had apparently turned off the security cameras last night, after he'd told everyone they could go home. Herb asked me why my father would do that. I told him I had no idea. I explained that I got locked in the store overnight. Herb said he could understand how it happened, because my dad rushed everyone out the door last night."

"Why would he do that?" Jennifer asked disbelievingly.

"I don't know. Frankly, Herb and I are both worried my father may be acting strangely. That's why I swore Herb to secrecy. I don't want it getting out that my dad has gone off his rocker."

"Oh," Jennifer said, beginning to feel his concern. "So no cameras were running?"

"No. And I told Herb *I'd* gotten locked in the store, but I said nothing about you."

"Why did you ask for the tape, then?" she asked, still suspicious.

"Because I wanted to make sure the camera by the bed hadn't malfunctioned somehow and stayed on when all the rest were turned off. So I asked Herb for that tape and said I wanted to be sure I wasn't caught on camera sleeping in the buff. Herb got a kick out of that."

Jennifer wasn't sure whether to believe him or not. The whole story sounded so farfetched. "What about 'Stop the Press'? I heard you mention the show in your phone call. You said they might be interested."

"Yes, in a promotional idea I have for June. It had nothing to do with any tape. I thought of a new idea last night and decided to get people working on it right away." He studied her doubting eyes. "Look, I'll give you the tape Herb gave me. You can play it tonight and see for yourself. It's blank, because it was never used."

"How do I know you didn't switch it?"

He looked angry now. "Because I didn't! You honestly think I would seduce you to get us on tape to sell to tabloid TV? What kind of person do you think I am?"

"Having us on display in the window was your idea. Kisses that wind up on local newscasts were your idea. I figured maybe tabloid TV was just your next step."

"I didn't come up with the idea of *us* on display, just anonymous people. It was my father who—" He stopped short. "My dad seems to have had a hand in all of this, hasn't he?"

Jennifer could follow the line of Charles's thinking. His father had talked him into being the male mannequin in the window, and she had the feeling he'd selected her, too. And now he'd apparently had the store shut down quickly last night and had turned off the security cameras himself. Jennifer remembered now that she thought she'd seen him outside the window late last night. "You think...you don't think...?" She shook her head, deciding she must be crazy. But then she began to remember some of the things Jasper Derring had said to her about Charles and about herself.

"You think he might be trying to throw us together?" Charles asked, expressing the thought she'd been reluctant to utter. "Matchmaking?"

"But...why would he pick me for you? He likes me, but even so, I'm not from a well-to-do family or even highly educated. I'm not in your social or economic league."

Charles smiled to himself, rather enigmatically. "I'll have to ask him about all this when I see him. In the meantime," he said, looking directly at her now, "do you believe me when I say that we weren't taped last night?"

She hesitated, but then nodded. Charles's eye was caught by someone at the window, and Jennifer turned to see. Some young people with cameras were motioning to them and shouting.

"Throw more eggs!" they were saying, laughing.

"Now they want us to throw eggs at each other instead of kiss," Charles commented with amusement.

"I wonder if we'll make the news again tonight," Jennifer said with a sigh. "God, I'll be glad when this assignment is over." She wanted her old normal life back. She was tired of being a minor celebrity.

"I'm sorry you're not enjoying this more," Charles said. "You seemed to for a while."

"I did, but my fifteen minutes of fame are dragging on way too long. I'd like to be back in Housewares, selling pots and pans."

"Away from me?" he asked.

She hesitated and then made herself nod affirmatively. "Last night was a mistake. I was afraid it would all seem sordid in the cold light of day, and it does. I was even throwing eggs at you! It's all gone sour."

"It was just a misunderstanding about the camera and the tape," he said. "We've straightened that out. Why say it's gone sour?"

"Because it has. The magic is gone. You made love to me with a cracker thrown on the camera lens because you thought the camera was running! What if the camera *was* running and the cracker had fallen off? Then we would *really* have a tape to worry about! And all because we've been on public display for almost a week. People watch our every move. Maybe we developed crushes on each other because that's what our audience wanted. And then we acted on that passing attraction. Well, it's almost over now. And I'll be darn glad when it is." She turned away from him and blinked back tears.

The thing was—what made her cry—was she knew that for her, it wasn't a momentary fascination. Jennifer *was* truly in love, though she would never admit that to Charles or anyone else. Even if Jasper Derring was playing matchmaker—and with some success, too—she knew her affair with Charles wouldn't ever be anything more than an affair, and a brief one at that. Charles obviously hadn't been much affected by their lovemaking. He was already busy thinking about his next publicity campaign. Their night in the display bed was probably just one of his more unusual and amusing sexual encounters, and nothing more.

She remained cool toward him all day. Might as well start distancing herself from him, she'd decided. The sooner the better, so she wouldn't get weepy again on their last day in the window.

In the evening, as she was changing for the bedroom display, someone handed her a newspaper. On the front page was a photo of her throwing an egg at Charles. The column headline read Window Pair Have Lovers' Spat. As she walked to the display window, wearing a black silk nightgown and robe, she saw Charles outside the small door in the corridor. She showed the paper to him.

"*Lovers'* spat," he read. "How do they know?"

"You didn't tell some reporter—"

"No," he assured her. "Why would I do that? They probably don't know anything. 'Lovers' spat' is just a catchy phrase." He took a videocassette out of the large pocket of his robe. "Here, I brought this for you. Play it tonight when you get home."

"Oh, never mind," she told him, tired of the whole thing. "I believe you."

"No, play it," he insisted. "I want you to see for yourself, so there's no doubt in your mind."

Reluctantly, she took the tape. She sat on the bed reading for the remainder of the evening, though she'd selected a different book to read—a nonfiction one about the difficulties men and women have communicating with each other. No more romance novels for her! Charles, as usual, went through his exercise routines on the equipment. She noticed he was avoiding looking at her, as she was at him. Good, she thought, though his indifference hurt. But she needed to get used to it. Because after tomorrow—their last day as display models—their relationship would be over forever. He would go back to being president of Derring Brothers, and she would go back to being just another of his employees.

When she got home, she inserted the tape in her VCR and played it. She'd expected it to be blank, as Charles had promised. When Charles's face suddenly appeared on her TV screen, Jennifer was shocked.

8

"Hi, Jennifer," Charles said to her from the TV screen. He was dressed in the sweater and shirt he'd worn that day for the window display. "I know I promised you this tape would be blank—and it is, the rest of it anyway. Herb arranged for me to add this private message with the taping equipment they have in the security office. I can't talk long—I have to change into my tux."

Jennifer sat on the floor in front of her TV, mouth open as she listened.

On the screen, Charles bowed his head for a moment, then looked up again. "You've been distant toward me after our egg-throwing session this morning. I didn't know how to talk to you, so I decided to do it this way. First, about last night...I want to emphasize that, to me, what happened between us was real and beautiful, not a mistake. And not sordid in any way. I didn't plan it—certainly not for publicity. I'm sorry about the cracker on the camera. You're right, I was taking a chance. But I wanted you so much and..." He swallowed. "Well, I guess there's no excuse for it. But I never intended—the last thing I'd ever want—is to cause you any embarrassment. I respect you too much. I've always had a high regard for you. Maybe it didn't seem that way, with all the gibes and jokes, but I always thought you were a special person."

He took a long breath, looking perplexed, as if he'd run out of things to say for the moment but hadn't said all that he should. He glanced at his watch. "I have to get back to the window. I guess that's about all I wanted to tell you. I hope you'll forgive me if you're still angry with me. I'm not exactly sure why you've been distant, but I hope we can at least be friends again. Talk to me tomorrow, will you?"

He got up and in a second the TV went black, showing blank tape. Jennifer rewound the tape and played his message again, and then again. What was she to make of it? Of course, it was an apology, and she was willing to forgive him. But what did he mean that he'd always thought she was a special person, and that he wanted to be friends again? Friends! After their passionate, out-of-bounds lovemaking, he expected that they could just go back to being friends the way they used to be? Maybe that could work for him, but Jennifer didn't think she'd ever be able to look at him as a mere friend again.

They were ex-lovers. Why not be straightforward and call themselves that? Yes, she decided, that was the approach to take tomorrow when she talked to him as he'd asked her to. She'd forgive him, but she intended to make him be honest about their relationship, too.

Charles felt harried the next morning. The first thing he learned upon arriving at the store was that a local TV news crew was on its way to tape an interview with him and Jennifer, on this their last day on display together. The interview was set for midmorning and the TV crew apparently wanted to tape them in the window.

Meanwhile, he'd been trying to get hold of his father to ask him why he'd turned off the security cameras and sent everyone home that night. His father, however, seemed to be avoiding his phone calls.

And besides those things on his mind, Charles was worried about Jennifer. He wondered what her reaction to his taped message had been and how she would behave toward him when he saw her. He'd heard she'd arrived and was in makeup. He'd wait to talk to her in the display window, where they could be alone—so to speak.

When he'd changed into that morning's selection of blue sweater and Christmas tie, he went into the kitchen display window and waved at the crowd gathered outside, who cheered when they saw him. He found the cooking instructions left for them. Fortunately, that morning's breakfast did not include eggs. Oatmeal with raisins, dates and brown sugar was the selection, to be prepared in the microwave. He puttered about, measuring the oatmeal and water, wondering what was keeping Jennifer.

In a moment, she walked in, looking lovely in a flowing, cream-colored outfit with wide-legged pants and a tunic top. Her hair today had long, loose waves that tumbled over her shoulders. His eyes caught hers, and she stared at him for a second, ignoring or oblivious to the wild cheers of the crowd on the sidewalk.

She looked down, chewed her lip, then raised her eyes to his again and walked up to the counter to stand next to him. "I watched the tape," she told him, her manner deliberate and sincere. "Thank you for the trouble you went to and for the things you said. I forgive you for... for the part about the cracker. Our argument yesterday was my fault, too, because I jumped to the conclusion that a tape existed and that you were going to use it for publicity. My imagination got carried away. I'm sorry."

"That's all right!" he rushed to say, relieved that she was speaking to him and apparently no longer angry. "The whole thing was such a crazy situation, it was easy for things to get misinterpreted.''

"Yes." She nodded gravely. He didn't like the serious shadows in her green eyes. "But as for our being friends like we used to—well, we can't. We're ex-lovers, Charles. That's what we are now. You can't pretend what happened didn't happen and just go back to the way things were. We had a . . . a fling, a quickie affair. It's over. The morning after has come and gone. Let's call a spade a spade and try to go on from there.''

Charles drew his eyebrows together in confusion. Why did she say they were *ex*-lovers? Who said their affair was over already?

Unless that was the way *she* wanted it.

He exhaled and his shoulders slumped. Yes, that must be why she was talking this way. She didn't want it to continue. Charles felt lost for a moment. She started stirring the oatmeal flakes and water he'd measured into a bowl. Absently, he opened the box of raisins and tossed some in.

"That's enough," she said as he was about to throw in another handful.

"Sorry," he muttered, dropping the raisins in his hand back into the box. "A little goes a long way for you, doesn't it?"

"What do you mean?" she asked, stirring.

"Nothing." He swallowed. "So where do we 'go' from here?"

"Go?"

"You've called a spade a spade. What happens now?"

She bowed her head and silently carried the bowl to the microwave oven. After closing the door and setting the timer, she said, "I don't know. That's more up to you than me. You're the president. I'm the employee.''

"Don't give me that!" he said sharply.

Her eyes flared. ''Well, that's the case, isn't it? You're the one with the power here. You can fire me or keep me on. If you keep me as an employee, then it's up to you how we'll go on. You can ignore me and pretend it didn't happen, or keep me dangling as your mistress, or give me some pretty bauble as a kiss-off.''

Charles felt so angry he could have throttled her. He barely managed to keep his voice under control as he said, ''Why do you always make this out to be something sordid? This isn't the 1950s. I don't look on you as my backstairs mistress. In my mind, we're two equal adults who became attracted to each other and acted on their mutual desire.''

She stared at him, looking a trifle dumbfounded. The bell on the microwave rang, and she turned to take out the bowl of oatmeal. As she set it on the counter, he couldn't see her face anymore. Her voice sounded a bit choked as she said, ''Well, what do you think should happen next?''

Confound her, why couldn't she give him a straight answer? ''That's what I'm asking you!''

She turned and he could see tears glazing her eyes, heightening their green color. ''I don't know what should come next,'' she said, lifting her shoulders slightly. ''I've never done this before. You've broken up with lots of women—that's why I'm looking to you for guidance. You ought to know how it should end better than I.''

''Why are you talking in terms of endings?'' he asked, more gently now.

She seemed thoroughly confused as she blinked back tears. ''Well, what else is there? You want us to go on sleeping together? We had a close call with the one time we did it. If we continued, even if we were careful, people would find out eventually. They always do. We'd be the topic of gossip at every coffee break around here. It might undermine your authority with your other employees. Everyone would think I had a special 'in' with you or that I was getting special favors. I don't want to be in a situation like that. If you have any common sense, you won't want to be, either.''

Charles knew he and his common sense tended to part company whenever Jennifer was near. She'd given him similar cautions even before they'd made love, and he knew then that she was right. He'd slept with her anyway. And she still was right. If he continued sleeping with her, and she continued to be his employee, then it would indeed begin to have a sordid tinge. He didn't want her to be the subject of gossip. "I guess I ought to fire you," he murmured with irony.

"Maybe I ought to quit," she said.

"Jennifer—" he objected.

"I think I should. I ought to go back to college and get my degree.''

This statement took Charles off guard. "You're hoping to get your professor back?''

"No," she said softly, tears filling her eyes again. "I'm just . . . I need to get away from you.''

That was telling it like it is, he thought, taken aback. "Why, have I ruined your life?''

"You've changed it.'' She blinked away the tears and attempted to smile. "I'll always remember my one night of adventure with you. It may be the only one I'll ever have. But I have to move on. I have to get my bearings again and set a new course for myself.'' She shook her head. "I don't think I can do that if I stay here near you.''

Charles felt devastated. He had the feeling she cared for him, but that she had to leave him for her own good. Charles didn't know what to think, much less what to say. Why did she think he was so bad for her? Simply because he was her employer? Was that really the only reason? Charles didn't know and he felt ill thinking about it. He'd never chased a woman away before just from loving her.

The last thought echoed through his mind. He'd never loved a woman before, he realized. Not really. Not any of them. He could say that for certain now, because he could tell the difference. He'd never felt what he felt for Jennifer before, never been so addlepated and turned inside out. This was new and different, and damned confusing. And now, just as he was figuring out the depth of his feelings for Jennifer, she was ready to leave.

He tried to think it all through as they sat at the table and ate their oatmeal in silence. All at once, he was distracted by his aid, who popped his head through the small door at the back and told him the TV crew had arrived.

"TV crew?" Jennifer said, looking at Charles.

"Sorry, I forgot to mention it. A local TV news station wants to interview us."

"Oh, no," she moaned.

"You can let me do most of the talking," he told her.

"They probably are here for the romance angle," she said, looking unhappy. "How are we supposed to pretend?"

Charles didn't have an answer to give her. *He* didn't have to pretend to have romantic feelings, but obviously she did. "We'll muddle through somehow," he said.

A crew of three came in with their equipment, which they spent about fifteen minutes setting up. Their presence made the crowd outside grow even larger. Finally, as they were seated around the small kitchen table, Mike Holburn, a local newscaster, began his interview.

"You've been in the headlines all week," Mike said. "What's it like having people stare at you all day long?"

"Like living in the proverbial fishbowl," Charles said.

Jennifer nodded in agreement.

"You've been making your own breakfast and lunch each day," Mike commented with a grin. "Food been good?"

"Neither of us is an expert cook," Charles said. "But our aids behind the scenes spelled out instructions for us."

Mike turned to Jennifer. "Was it in the instructions to throw eggs at Mr. Derring yesterday?"

Jennifer looked numb for half a second, but then she blurted out, "That's how you scramble them in the shell."

Charles laughed along with Mike, marveling at her presence of mind.

"Some of the onlookers outside seemed to think you were throwing them at Mr. Derring for a different reason. They thought it looked more like a lovers' quarrel."

Charles answered this time, wanting to spare Jennifer. "That's because the crowd keeps hoping for some excitement and they get inventive."

"All of Chicago has been wondering if there's a romance going on between you, beginning with that news conference you gave," Mike said. "*Is* there a romance going on here in Derring Brothers' windows?"

As Jennifer lowered her eyes, Charles grew quiet for a moment, considering how to answer. "Let's say I'd like there to be one."

Mike perked up. "You would? You mean—"

"That's my statement," Charles said, heading him off. "I have nothing more to add."

Mike turned to the surprised-looking young woman sitting between them. "Jennifer?"

She blinked. "I . . . have nothing more to add, either."

"Well!" Mike seemed pleased with what they weren't saying. "Today's your last day in the windows. Are you glad it's over, or do you wish it could last longer?"

He pointed the microphone at Jennifer first. "I'm kind of glad it's over," she said, looking shy now. "I'm not used to being in the public eye."

When Mike turned the microphone on him, Charles said, "I've enjoyed the experience more than I ever thought I would. In fact, I'm planning another window display for June."

Mike grew animated. "Really? Will you be in that one, too?"

"It all depends," Charles replied, the camera and lights giving him impetus to take steps in the direction he wanted to go, hoping Jennifer would follow.

"On what?" Mike asked.

"On whether Jennifer's willing to share the window with me again. I wouldn't go on display with anyone else," Charles said, taking on a tongue-in-cheek air.

Mike pounced on Jennifer again with his microphone. "Would you be willing to do this again, Jennifer?"

Poor Jennifer looked confounded. "I . . . I'll wait until June to decide."

"Oh, no, you won't," Charles said under his breath, feeling his oats.

Mike picked up on the comment. "What was that?" He pointed the microphone at Charles.

"That was me talking to myself. Bad habit of mine."

"Right," Mike said, laughing. He turned to the camera. "That's the latest from the Derring Brothers display windows. We'll keep you posted on Jennifer's decision."

When Mike and his crew had packed up, Mike thanked them and shook hands, then walked out, closing the small door behind him. Still near the door, away from the window and the crowd, Jennifer said to Charles, "Why did you say that about another window display in June? You know I wouldn't do this again. I told you, I'm leaving Derring Brothers."

"You haven't left yet," Charles said. "Therefore, there's still hope."

"You want me to stay?"

"Of course I want you to stay."

"Why? Isn't it easier for us both if I leave?"

"It wouldn't be easier for me," he said.

"Why?" She touched her fingertips to her mouth. "Wh-why did you tell him that you would like there to be a romance between us? Are you just trying to milk this for all the publicity you can squeeze out of it?"

"No, Jenny. I'm not thinking of the publicity. I'm thinking of you and me."

"What about the June promotion you're planning, that you won't be in unless I'm in the window with you? You're just cashing in on the success of this Christmas display and hoping you can make it work again in six months. Well, I won't do it! And don't give me any more of that 'I'm just thinking of you and me' bit. I'm not as gullible as I was a week ago!"

"Jennifer—" He tried to catch her arm, but she yanked it away, out of his reach.

Her back against the small door now, she said, "Don't touch me! Honestly, I don't know what you want from me." Her hands and voice were shaking now. He felt badly because she was so upset. "I've cooperated with this display thing from the beginning, even though I never wanted to do it," she told him, edging away when he tried to approach her again. "I just sat through a TV interview trying to answer embarrassing questions. I went along with the idea of having a romance with you because that was what people seemed to want. I even slept with you! Now you expect me to stick around and do this all over again in

June? What about me? What about my feelings in all this? I'm not an actress. I can't play a part I don't feel anymore!''

He was about to try to take her in his arms and comfort her, but her last comment cut him to the quick. He took a step backward.

"All right!" he said, a lump in his throat making his voice rough. "Go then. Leave tomorrow. I'll write up a nice recommendation for you."

She nodded, sniffing back tears. "Thank you. I'm... sorry it ended like this."

Charles didn't say anything aloud, but his heart was shouting, *It hasn't ended yet, Jenny!*

"I can leave tomorrow?" she asked, disrupting his thoughts. "Or must I give two weeks' notice?"

"Two weeks' notice would be appreciated, but I don't want to keep you here any longer than you can stand it," he said in a sarcastic tone, looking at her tear-smudged eyes. Again, he longed to hold her in his arms and soothe her, but he knew she wouldn't let him, and that knowledge stung. After a glance at his watch, he said, "It's time for a break. Go get your eye makeup touched up."

"All right." She stared at him, her eyes going through him like a sword. "You're angry with me now, aren't you?"

"Yes," he replied, but the truth was that he was feeling a lot more than anger. He wished he had time to sort his brain out. It was giving him too many messages at once. *Make her stay. Tell her you don't give a damn if she leaves. Tell her you want her. Don't lose your pride. Don't lose her!*

"I never wanted to make you angry," she said, looking so sincere he thought his heart would break. "I can't handle this situation anymore, that's all. You've... it's been too much for me. I know you'd like us to be friends, but I can't. I'm sorry you're disappointed.''

The way she was looking at him now, he could almost swear she cared for him, maybe even was in love with him. She wanted him to think well of her, he realized. Maybe he could use that to buy a little time, until he could figure himself out and hatch some kind of plan to get her to stay.

"Get your eyes fixed," he said coolly.

Her face grew crestfallen and she turned and rushed out the small door. He followed, wanting to call her back and tell her he hadn't meant to speak so curtly. But he ran into someone else just outside the door—his father.

"Dad! Where have you been? I've been trying—"

"Yes, I know. I've been dodging your calls. You've made a pretty mess of things, haven't you?"

Charles shook his head, not sure he'd heard correctly. "Of what? The publicity campaign's been a huge success.''

"I'm not talking about that." Jasper looked around, eyeing a passing employee nearby. "Let's go to your dressing room. I want to talk to you in private."

As they walked to Charles's dressing room in the men's department, Charles wondered what was upsetting his father. He realized that Jasper had been close enough to the door to perhaps overhear his conversation with Jennifer.

When they reached the dressing room, Jasper dismissed Charles's aids and other employees and closed the door.

"You're letting Jennifer quit?" Jasper said.

"That's what she wants." Charles knew for sure now that Jasper had heard what they'd said.

"Is that what you want?" Jasper quizzed him.

"No!"

"Well, so do something about it!"

"Like what?" Charles asked, looking for a good suggestion.

"Tell her you want her to stay."

"I did."

Jasper, though much shorter than Charles, always seemed able to look him in the eye on an equal level, and he did so now, with vehemence. "Then tell her you love her!"

Charles stared at him. It wasn't the first time his father seemed to know Charles's mind better than he did himself. It was funny how in one's teens and early twenties, parents seemed out of touch and a little slow. And then later, they somehow became smart again. "How do you know I love her?" Charles asked quietly.

"I've known that since you worked with her in Housewares. Why do you think I arranged to have you locked in the store together overnight? If I left things up to you, you'd never figure out which side of your bread is buttered."

Charles looked at his father keenly, beginning to smile. "I knew that was what you were up to, ever since they told me you turned off the security cameras. You were watching us outside through the window, and you saw that Jennifer had lost her earring—"

"And I went back in, told everyone still there to go home and said I would close the place up. And I did—with you two still in the window. I couldn't have thought of a better opportunity if I tried! And it fell into my lap—that's fate for you. But what have you done with the opportunity? Botched it up completely!"

"There was a misunderstanding. She thought we were taped and—"

"Misunderstandings can usually be worked out if you just talk it over."

"We did," Charles insisted. "We straightened it all out. I apologized. She accepted the apology, and apologized to me. We're all hunky-dory about that. But . . . she seems to want our romance to be over. How can I make her stay if she doesn't want me?"

"Women like to hear the word *love*. Have you used it yet?"

Charles lowered his eyes. "No. I . . . I've only just been realizing in the past day or two that that was how I felt. I've never told anyone that before. But what if *she* doesn't love *me*? I don't think she does. At least she doesn't say so."

Jasper shook his head in dismay. "Charles, don't let pride get in the way. Just as you do in business, you've got to take risks."

Charles nodded. "But she seems to be in kind of a confused state of mind right now. Like me."

"That's what being in love is like at first. It's normal. Don't worry about it."

"If I tell her I love her, she might misinterpret it, think I'm saying it to keep her around for publicity purposes. Or she might misinterpret what she's feeling and give the wrong answer. I don't think it's a discussion we should have in the display window with everyone watching."

"You're right about that. Find some time alone with her."

"Yeah, but when? We're here till ten. She'll rush home. I'll have to wait until tomorrow, and that makes me nervous. I'm not altogether certain she'll show up for work tomorrow, even though she offered to give two weeks' notice. She's so determined to escape me, I'm afraid she'll disappear on me—not answer my phone calls—maybe even leave town." An idea came into Charles's mind as he gazed at his father. He had a feeling that telepathy was at work between them. "If I can arrange to lose something in the window tonight, can you arrange to..."

"Lock you in the store again?" Jasper raised his chin and grinned. "I think I can manage it."

"Can you unlock my office door and leave it open?"

"You bet."

Charles exhaled. "Good. I'll try to manage the rest." He scrutinized his father's lined face and ever-alert eyes. "How did you know I loved her?"

"By the way you couldn't stop sparring with her, or take your eyes off her. And don't worry. She loves you, too. She lights up and her voice gets higher whenever you're around."

"I never noticed."

"Your senses have been clouded by all those women who threw themselves at you. Jennifer's a lady, and other than your mother, I'm not sure you've ever met one before. Women who have a natural modesty and refinement need closer scrutiny. You'll learn."

Charles had to marvel at his father's point of view on things—old-fashioned, but down to earth and true. He grinned. "You're a kick and a half, you know?"

"That's what you'll get from me if you don't convince Jennifer to be your wife."

"Wife? Oh, I see. I'm to marry her, too."

Jasper eyed him darkly. "Don't you want to?"

Charles took a breath. "Yes! Now that you mention it. I hadn't thought that far ahead yet. Right now, I'm just hoping to get her to love me."

"Hadn't thought that far? What about the wedding display you want to do in June?"

"How do you know about that already?"

"I keep up with things," Jasper said. "What put the idea of a wedding into your head?"

"Oh, June, moon, croon. It's what June is famous for, weddings."

"And you want to do the display with Jennifer?"

"Yes, but she doesn't want to." Charles scratched his nose. "Of course, I didn't mention that it had to do with a wedding."

Jasper shook his head. "You're some piece of work! I'm betting that the whole reason you even thought of the idea of a wedding display with Jennifer is because you..." He waved his fingers, wanting Charles to finish his sentence.

"I want to marry her." Charles threw up his hands. "Okay, okay, you're right. Lock me up with her so she can't escape me, and I'll propose!"

"Good," Jasper said, looking pleased for once. "I'll talk to your mother about booking a place to have the reception. You'll need to set a date. Why not June? Or even April or May?"

"Dad..."

"Think about it. I'm off!"

Charles watched as Jasper rushed off to do his new errands. He wanted to warn his father that it might not happen the way they wanted it to. Jennifer might say *no*. Jennifer might spit in Charles's eye and tell him he was crazy. Well, one thing was right. Charles *was* crazy. Crazy in love, and totally spinning—and on the verge of unending happiness or heartbreak, all depending on what one beautiful, green-eyed young woman said.

9

—➤—

Jennifer sat up in bed reading, or trying to, wearing a long, lavender satin-and-lace peignoir. She hadn't spoken much to Charles all evening, and she avoided looking at him while he performed his nightly routine on the equipment. She didn't want to be reminded of how physically devastating he looked and how much she still desired him. Since it was nearing ten o'clock, the crowd outside was smaller, but faithful. Earlier, one group of four women had held up a homemade sign that read Better Than The Soaps! We'll Miss You!!

Just before 10:00 p.m., Charles finished his final workout stretches. He began pacing all around the display, the carpeting and the furniture, apparently searching for something.

"What are you looking for?" she asked, putting down her book.

"I lost one of the cuff links I wore with my tux tonight. It was solid gold."

"Maybe you lost it in the dressing room when you changed," she said.

"No," he replied, peering under the bed now, near her. "That's when I noticed it was missing, and my assistant and I searched the dressing room." He lifted another edge of the bedspread and peeked under it. "We couldn't find it, so I must have lost it in the window." He glanced up at her from his kneeling position. "Want to help me look?"

"Sure," she said with a sigh. "But only for a minute. I don't want to get stuck overnight again."

"How could something like that happen twice?" Charles asked. "Besides, we'll find it more quickly if we both look."

Jennifer got off the bed and began searching the carpeting and furnishings, too. Then a thought crossed her mind. She stood up straight and said, "Wait a minute. If you dropped the cuff link while you were wearing the tux, then you would have lost it in the living room display, not here in the bedroom."

Charles, on his hands and knees, paused and nodded in agreement, though she noticed he didn't seem to want to meet her eyes. "You're right! Stupid of me. Why didn't I think of that? Well, we'd better go over to the next window and search there."

He rose to his feet, took her by the hand, and led her out of the bedroom display and through the small corridor in back of checkout counters that led to the next window. She quickly glanced around and noticed no one was nearby.

"Charles, the place looks empty already!" she exclaimed, pulling on his hand. "Why don't we search tomorrow? I want to get out of here before they lock the doors!"

Charles paused, keeping hold of her hand, and surveyed the store. She followed his gaze as he looked at the large revolving entrance doors. The doors stood still now and were perfectly aligned—as if locked.

"They haven't closed up already, have they?" She pulled her hand out of his and ran to one of the doors and tried to move it. "It's locked!" She looked at her watch. "It's only two minutes after ten. *Someone* must still be here to let us out," she said frantically. She ran down the broad center aisle that led to the escalators. "Hello? Anybody here?" No one answered. The empty store had the same mysterious, spooky aura that it had the night when she and Charles had gotten locked in.

She tensed in shock when someone came up from behind and took hold of her shoulders.

"It's no use," Charles said. "We're locked in again."

"But how could it happen?" she asked, turning to glare at him. "You said yourself such a thing couldn't happen twice." She noted the tentative, yet slightly smug look in his eyes, and suddenly two and two added up to four. "*You* did this! You arranged this! Your cuff link wasn't missing, was it?"

"No," he admitted calmly.

"You ... you bastard!" she said, pressing her hands against his chest, trying to give him a shove. Her effort had no effect. Instead, he took hold of her hands and kept them clasped to his rib cage. "Why?" she asked. "Just to get me in bed again?"

"So we would have some time alone together to talk," he said in a soothing tone.

"Well, why didn't you just ask to talk to me? Why have us locked up overnight again?"

"Because I was afraid you'd run off. You've hardly talked to me since the interview this morning. I knew you wouldn't listen to me."

She pulled her hands from his grasp. "What is it that you have to say?" she asked coldly, turning her back to him.

"Would you look at me?"

"No!"

She heard him exhale. "How can we talk if we can't see each other's eyes?"

"I can hear you," she said. "I don't want to look at you! You deliberately got us locked in here for another long night, all so you could seduce me again. Well, it won't work!" She tied her robe more tightly around her.

"I'm not trying to seduce you!" he said with impatience. "I'm trying to tell you I love you, damn it!"

Love me, she thought with astonishment. What kind of new trick was this? "What do you mean, you love me?" she asked coolly, afraid to turn and face him.

"I love you," he repeated. "I'm wild about you, can't stop thinking about you and wanting you. I've only just realized it in the past couple of days, but I've been in love with you for a long time."

"You have?" Shyly, she turned to look at him.

His eyes were bright blue and shining with intensity. "Yes!" He stepped closer and took hold of her upper arms. "I'm so in love I don't know what to do. I think we should get married."

The joy budding in Jennifer's heart faded and vanished. She shook her head slowly. "No, Charles. We could never marry. That's ridiculous. How could you even consider—"

"Ridiculous!" Charles repeated, a harrowed look in his eyes. "Why? You don't love me?"

"Because we come from two different worlds. You're wealthy and one of Chicago's most prominent businessmen. I'm just a middle-class girl who never finished college. How could I ever fit into your social circle?"

Charles half closed his eyes, exhaling in an effort to be patient. Then he gave her a gentle shake. "Don't be silly! You can always finish college if you want to. As for my upper-class social circles," he said with irony, "my father thinks you're the classiest woman I've ever met. And so do I. We Derrings may have money, but we're not all that sophisticated. Look at my father—he was the one who locked us in the store together the first time, hoping proximity would make the sparks fly between us. In my mind, that's a pretty salty thing to do. But it worked—sparks flew. When we were alone together, it didn't matter what our bank accounts added up to or who our friends were. All we wanted was each other.''

Jennifer felt strangely heartened, but was still afraid to hope. ''I'm confused. You never mentioned or even hinted at marriage before—not even after we'd made love. I never thought of it as a possibility. How did you decide all of a sudden that you wanted to marry me?''

''Let me try to unconfuse you. I've only just straightened it out in my own mind.'' He smiled and ran his hands warmly up and down her arms. ''The living window-display promotion has gone so well, it was a natural business move to think about repeating the success by having another one. The idea came to me—it was the day we got locked in—that a wedding display window in June would attract the public. At first I figured that we'd hire professional models or choose an engaged couple from our bridal registry. But then I started thinking maybe I should do the display again to attract extra attention. And when I thought about whom I'd want to play my bride in the mock wedding, I knew you were the only one I'd want for the role. After we'd made love, I began to realize that I didn't want it to be a mock wedding. I wanted it to be real! A conversation with my father this morning made that crystal clear in my mind. I admit I've been a little mixed up about my feelings all week. But the confusion is all gone now, and I know my own mind better than I ever have in my life. I want *you* to be my *wife.*'' He gazed at her with agonized anticipation in his eyes. ''What do you say?''

This was crazy, she thought. She felt a bit angry with him. Tears filled her eyes. "Yes, I'll marry you!" she said, blinking hard so she could see him clearly. "But if you think I'll go along with having our wedding in a display window, think again!"

The trepidation in Charles's face disappeared into a broad, happy smile. Laughing, he took her in his arms. "No, Jenny, I won't turn our wedding ceremony into a publicity stunt. I was just explaining how I came to realize that I wanted to marry you."

"But you told that TV newsman this morning that you wanted me to do the June display window with you," she reminded him, wiping away slightly hysterical tears of happiness.

"I know," he said. "I hadn't thought that through. I was trying to win you back, trying to give you clear signals that I wanted you around. Although—" he paused thoughtfully "—I didn't tell him that the June display would have to do with weddings. We could always make it some other type of display—maybe for vacations and travel... honeymoons. Would you do it with me for one day? Pretend to pour over travel books and pack luggage? We can do it after we're married."

"After?" she said. "We'll be married by June?"

"My father's off setting the date right now."

"What?" she said, laughing.

"Our suspicions were correct. He's been playing matchmaker all along. He arranged to lock us in the store again tonight—though this time it was my idea, not his. But he was happy to assist."

Jennifer shook her head in astonishment. "And I thought *you* were the most incorrigible person I'd ever met."

"Where do you think I got it from? Dad's been after me to find a wife for years now. I ignored him. I guess he finally decided to do something about it."

"But why did he pick me?"

Charles's eyes glowed with playful lights. "He said he could tell we were in love when we worked together in Housewares. I know that now, but I had no clue then how I felt about you. Did you?"

"No. I didn't think you could ever love me."

"I mean," Charles said, looking uneasy again, "did you know you loved me?"

"Then?" She paused to consider the question, trying to remember her state of mind at the time. "I probably knew, but I wouldn't let myself even think about it. I thought you'd never choose me. You always dated such glamorous women."

"So you *were* in love with me then?"

"Yes," she whispered. "I was."

"And now?" His eyes hovered on hers, waiting for her answer.

She realized he still wasn't sure of her feelings. "I love you more than ever," she told him, a new glaze of tears blurring his face as she looked at him. "I finally admitted it to myself after we spent the night together. Only, I thought it was just a brief fling, something to tide you over after Delphine ran off. I remember thinking, For me this is real, but for him, it's just a passing yen—born of a publicity stunt." She hesitated, felt her lips tremble. "Are you sure it isn't only that, Charles?"

"I'm positive," he assured her, pulling her to him and kissing her forehead. "I've never felt like this before in my life. I've been panicked all day, fearing I was about to lose you. You give me the feeling that there's a foundation under me, that I'm not just skimming the surface anymore.

I'm ready to give up looking at life as if it was one long party and I'm eager to make plans for a nice, long, steady marriage instead. That's what I want now, and you're the only woman with whom I can have that."

His words made her face crumple. "I never thought I'd hear you say that." She wept into his shoulder. "I'm so happy."

"I wish you *looked* happier," he said, giving her an extra squeeze. "Don't cry. How about giving me a kiss instead?"

She smiled, wiped away her tears with her hands, and tilted her face to meet his as he bent his head. They kissed tenderly, full of gentle warmth and mutual reassurance. But as she slipped her arms around his neck and he pressed her against him, their kiss became even warmer and soon grew hot with desire. His hand moved between them, found its way through folds of satin and lace to her soft flesh. He fondled her breast and teased her nipple. She responded by kissing him with increasing ardor. She pulled away from his lips and pressed her hand on his over her breast.

"Are the security cameras turned off?" she asked.

"I don't know," Charles said. "I didn't cover that point with my father." His eyes, liquid with sensuality, brightened. "I asked him to leave my office door open. There are no security cameras there. And there's a big leather couch—"

"Let's go," she responded, her voice showing her ache of desire.

By the time they'd climbed ten floors, both were out of breath. They went into his office and sat down on the couch. He didn't even give her a chance to catch her breath. He pushed away her robe, revealing the low-cut, lace-topped nightgown that barely covered her heaving breasts.

"You're exquisite," he murmured, moving his fingertips over the top of the lace. She could feel their heat gliding over her skin. He slipped his hand beneath the lace and she closed her eyes with pleasure. She gasped when he pushed the gown off her shoulders, fully exposing her. He pressed his face between her breasts, hotly kissing her skin.

She breathed haltingly, her voice unsteady. "I was resigned to the idea that we'd never do this again.... Ohh, Charles...I love the way you love me." As he sucked hard on her nipple, she moaned softly, feeling electric sensations shooting to another part of her body.

His mouth left her breast, and he kissed her neck insistently, then returned to her mouth. "You respond so sweetly," he murmured. "I was afraid I'd never know your love again." As they rose upward together in another kiss, he pushed the satin nightgown down her waist, past her hips. She squirmed out of it and dropped it on the floor. He made short work of the satin bikini panties that remained, ripping the tiny side seam so that his fingers could seek out the point that ached for his touch.

Jennifer moaned wantonly, her desire instantly flaming into a blazing torch. She unfastened the waistband of his pajamas, freeing the hardness of his erection. He reclined on the couch and urged her to climb on top of him. As she straddled him, she took the thick length of him inside her. They began slow up and down movements, and then he pulled her toward him, bringing her breasts to his face. These he kissed and suckled until she almost sobbed from the need building in her body, hungrily demanding satisfaction.

"You're so sexy!" he breathed. "I could lose my mind, the way you turn me on."

She ripped open the buttons of his pajama top, so she could see and feel his broad, muscled chest. She leaned downward and grazed his skin with her breasts, then sat up in delicious shock, as he slipped his fingers between them and touched the quick of her again.

"Charles!" she cried, heart pounding. "Oh, Charles...!" She grew delirious from the torrid sensations, felt her stomach muscles tensing deep inside. He increased the back-and-forth movement within her and she responded with equal energy, until they writhed in shared exquisite torture. She cried out his name again and threw her head back as a huge spasm tore through her body, and then another and another. When they subsided, she breathed again, feeling slightly dizzy. After she recovered, she looked at him, and his eyes were bright with adoration for her alone. Limp, tearful with joy, she lay down on his chest. Soon she could feel him climax inside her as he held her tightly in his arms.

Neither spoke for a long moment, recovering.

Eventually, she kissed him and smiled. "We can keep on doing this now—as often as we want, can't we?"

He gave her an extra squeeze. "Often, and forever."

The next morning, after a blissful night on the couch with Jennifer in his arms, Charles showered in the executive men's room and dressed in a new suit he picked up in the men's department. Jennifer, he assumed, had done the same, though he hadn't seen her since she'd disappeared into the executive ladies' room.

Soon it was opening time, and employees began to show up for work. Charles tried to tone down his natural exuberance from the night before and look calm and everydayish. Though he longed to, he knew he ought not to advertise that he'd just lived through the best night of his entire life.

All at once, his father came through his office door, surprising him. Charles took his feet off his desk and sat more properly in his chair. "Hi, Dad!"

"Well?"

"It's settled," he told his father with pride. "She's going to marry me."

"Congratulations! You don't know how happy I am, and how relieved your mother will be, to hear that. This news is the best Christmas present we've ever had."

"Thanks for your help," Charles said, "even if you are a conniving old busybody!" He instantly wished he'd watched his language, because Jennifer suddenly walked in. She wore a marvelous green wool suit that matched her eyes. He noticed that she was also wearing some makeup and her hair was as wavy as a silken waterfall. This was curious, since Mr. James and the hairdresser had finished their duties yesterday. Jennifer must have made herself up this morning, and she looked absolutely perfect.

But he quickly noticed that she had a serious, tentative demeanor, which made his stomach tighten. He hoped she wasn't having second thoughts.

"Good morning, Mr. Derring," she said politely, and rather shyly, to his father.

Jasper smiled and shook her hand warmly. "Good morning!"

She turned and looked at Charles in a very formal, direct manner. "I'm giving you my two weeks' notice."

Alarmed, Charles stood up. "No, Jenny! Why?"

Her brows drew together and she seemed befuddled. "Because...well, under the circumstances..." She glanced hesitantly at Jasper. "I don't think I should continue working here."

Charles moved his eyes back and forth over her face, trying to read what was in her mind. He leaned over the desk between them. "You mean, because we're engaged, you shouldn't work here anymore?"

She nodded.

Charles exhaled with relief. "You scared the bejeebers out of me! I thought you'd changed your mind about marrying me."

Jennifer cupped her hand over her mouth and started laughing. "I'm sorry. I wasn't sure if I was supposed to go back to work today as usual, or what." Again, she glanced at Jasper.

Charles began to realize she felt unsure of his father, perhaps still finding it hard to believe that his parents would really accept her into their family and uncertain how to behave around him.

Jasper seemed to pick up on this, too. "Keeping Charles guessing is good for him," he told Jennifer with a wink. "But he's too young to have a heart attack like me, so try not to shake him up too much, will you?"

Jennifer looked embarrassed. "I will...won't..." She chuckled at her own confusion.

"My dear, Charles's mother is looking forward to meeting you," Jasper said. "I've told her a lot about you, and she's seen you on TV, too. She thinks you're perfect for Charles, as do I."

Jennifer's color heightened a bit. "I hope you both won't be disappointed."

Jasper took her hand and said, "You haven't disappointed me yet. When I saw you two in Housewares, I thought, now there's the sort of woman Charles ought to be taking up with, instead of the pampered debutantes who flaunt themselves to get his attention. I want my children to marry people who weren't born with a silver spoon in their mouths and know the value of hard work. I didn't come from wealth and neither did my wife. But our children did, and unfortunately, my wife and I spoiled them. We've realized that too late."

"Really!" Charles said, amused.

Jasper glanced at Charles, smiled, and looked at Jennifer again. "Charles is the most stable and levelheaded of my children, so you needn't be alarmed by what I'm saying. But you'll be a good influence on him, because he'll pay more attention to your inborn wisdom than he ever did to my attempts to advise him. So, in short, you're a very welcome addition to the Derring family."

A sheen of moisture filled Jennifer's eyes, but she blinked quickly and smiled. "Thank you, Mr. —"

"Call me Jasper... or Dad, if you like." Jasper's dark eyes had a new light to them. He was happier than Charles had seen him in the past several years. Charles hadn't realized how much his father worried about his children, even now when they were all grown and on their own.

"Jasper, for now," Jennifer said. "I'm grateful to you for playing matchmaker. Otherwise, Charles and I might never have realized how we felt about each other."

Jasper looked pleased with himself. "I thought that if you two had to spend a week together in such close quarters, you'd figure out you were in love. And true love won out—with just a little extra nudge from me. I guess you know by now that I locked you two in the store."

"A brilliant move," Charles said. "Though Herb in Security thinks you've gone batty."

"I've already set him straight," Jasper said. He glanced at his briefcase. "Before I forget, I have something to show you." He opened the case and took out what looked like a piece of needlework.

"Did Mom make that?" Charles asked, trying to get a look at the fabric as Jasper took it out and turned it right side up.

"No, I did," Jasper said. "I haven't advertised the fact that I took up needlepoint when I was recovering from my heart attack. Some people might think I'd turned sissy. But I'm anxious for you to see." He held it up and pointed out the names he'd stitched in. "I've been working on this with you two in mind for months. The empty space is left for the wedding date. I need your help on that so I can finish this and have it made into a pillow for you."

"That's so sweet!" Jennifer exclaimed, looking touched and excited. "You had that much faith that we would eventually get married?"

Jasper quirked his mouth. "Not so much faith as blind hope against hope. Frankly, I was afraid Charles might never marry. Until a few days ago, he's never shown the slightest interest in the state of matrimony."

Charles rolled his head to one side and listened patiently to his parent rail on.

"Concentrating on stitching this wedding pillow was a way of putting the idea of you two being married out into the universe. I hoped if I kept a positive attitude about it as I worked each stitch that God would somehow make things fall into place. It's the first time I've tried such a notion. But it seems to have worked." He blinked and murmured, "I wonder if it would work as well with my other children."

"That's lovely," Jennifer said with obvious sincerity. "We'll treasure it always."

Charles found himself on the verge of choking down a trace of nausea. It was bad enough his father had turned himself into a professional matchmaker, but now he'd invented needlepoint voodoo to try to control the universe.

Not that Charles was sorry his methods had worked. But he felt as though he ought to warn his siblings about Dad. Then again, maybe not. Since he was so happy, why shouldn't he wish the same for his brothers and sister?

"So," Jasper said, "what about the date?"

Jennifer looked at Charles and said, "We hadn't thought much about that yet."

"No, but Dad has," Charles reminded her. "He mentioned June."

"Yes, June," Jasper said. "But how about April instead? The reception will be at our home, so that's no problem."

"I'm sure it'll be beautiful," Jennifer said.

"It's the caterers and lining up the church that's tricky," Jasper explained. "My wife and I called a few places and it looks like the second Saturday of April works best. That suit you?"

"Sure," Jennifer said, smiling.

"You mean we have a choice?" Charles said, teasing his father.

"Of course you have a choice," Jasper said, quirking his mouth. "You can have the second Saturday or the day after the second Friday. I know what you're thinking, Charles, and I don't mean to plan your wedding for you. But the thing is, Jennifer has no living parents to give her a wedding. You have the store to run, and Jennifer will be busy buying her trousseau, so I'm making myself available to help."

Charles's shoulders shook with amusement. "Sounds fine to me."

"Great!" Jasper said. Carefully, he put the needlepoint back in his briefcase. "I'll be able to finish this now." He closed the case and glanced at them. "Why don't you two take some time off today? You've been cooped up in the windows for a week. Spend the day...doing what you like," he said with a sly grin. "Though I can't imagine what that would be." His dark eyes glistened and Charles could almost read what was on his mind—grandchildren. "Well, I'm off!" Jasper told them.

Jennifer and Charles said goodbye and watched him walk out the door. Charles closed it behind him so they could have some privacy. He took Jennifer in his arms. "Think you'll be able to tolerate such a busybody for a father-in-law?"

Jennifer chuckled. "I've always liked Jasper. And once we're married, he'll probably turn his attention to marrying off his other children."

"That's true," Charles said. "Speaking of marriage, I got a letter from Delphine in yesterday's mail."

"Delphine? What did she have to say?"

"She and the professor were married in Nevada a few days ago."

"Married!" Jennifer looked astonished.

Charles let go of her to pick the letter up off his desk. "They beat us! How do you like that?" Charles commented, showing it to Jennifer. "At least it all worked out for everyone."

Jennifer read the letter and smiled in a philosophical sort of way. "I'm glad. I hope they'll be happy. But who would have guessed that those two would make a pair?"

"Who would have guessed we would?" Charles countered, taking her hand. "So...should we follow my dad's advice and take the day off?"

"Can you?"

"I can arrange it."

"Where should we go? What will we do?" she asked, straightening his tie.

"Anything you want," he said, his voice growing earthy.

"In that case," she said with a little grin, "we don't have to go anywhere. The couch was so comfortable last night. All we need to do is lock the door."

"My staff might think it's a little odd," Charles said, fiddling with the top button of her suit.

"So what else is new? I've already heard gossip this morning. Some people are speculating about why everyone was asked to leave early last night. Seems they noticed us still in the window when they left. And they remembered that other time, too, so. . ."

"So, we might as well do what they think we're doing?" he asked.

"Why not? I'm not an employee anymore," she whispered, an ardent gleam in her eyes that made his heart pound.

Charles went around her and locked the door. "Okay, just this once during business hours, because you've got me too hot and bothered to say no. But afterward, I think we should leave and have a long lunch somewhere and spend the afternoon at my place."

Jennifer grinned. "I always thought I was a straitlaced prude and that I'd live a boring life. And now I'm seducing the president of Derring Brothers on company time and making plans to marry him! It's like a...a slightly naughty fairy tale come true."

"And my dad is the fairy godmother!" He took her in his arms. "Well, who cares, as long as I can live out your slightly naughty fairy tale with you." He nibbled her ear and kissed her smooth, delicate jawbone. "I especially like the naughty part...."

* * * * *

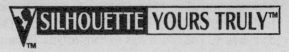

SILHOUETTE YOURS TRULY™

Sneak Previews of March titles,
from Yours Truly

It Happened One Week by JoAnn Ross
Amanda Stockenberg was in the middle of the worst
week of her life, looking like something the cat dragged
in and acting rather unladylike, when she saw *him*. Her
first love. And now she has only seven days for a second
chance at forever....

What *Engagement Ring?!* by Martha Schroeder
April Kennan had refused to even *date* attorney
Jake Singleton's brother, let alone marry him, but he
insists she broke their engagement and kept a four-carat
diamond ring! Now Jake's demanding she return a ring
she'd never been given—or else!

As seen on TV!
Free Gift Offer

With a Free Gift proof-of-purchase from any Silhouette® book,
you can receive a beautiful cubic zirconia pendant.

This gorgeous marquise-shaped stone is a genuine cubic
zirconia—accented by an 18" gold tone necklace.

(Approximate retail value $19.95)

Send for yours today...
compliments of *Silhouette*®

To receive your free gift, a cubic zirconia pendant, send us one original proof-of-purchase, photocopies not accepted, from the back of any Silhouette Romance™, Silhouette Desire®, Silhouette Special Edition®, Silhouette Intimate Moments® or Silhouette Shadows™ title available in February, March or April at your favorite retail outlet, together with the Free Gift Certificate, plus a check or money order for $1.75 U.S./$2.25 CAN. (do not send cash) to cover postage and handling, payable to Silhouette Free Gift Offer. We will send you the specified gift. Allow 6 to 8 weeks for delivery. Offer good until April 30, 1996 or while quantities last. Offer valid in the U.S. and Canada only.

Free Gift Certificate

Name: _____

Address: _____

City: _____ State/Province: _____ Zip/Postal Code: _____

Mail this certificate, one proof-of-purchase and a check or money order for postage and handling to: SILHOUETTE FREE GIFT OFFER 1996. In the U.S.: 3010 Walden Avenue, P.O. Box 9057, Buffalo NY 14269-9057. In Canada: P.O. Box 622, Fort Erie,

---

FREE GIFT OFFER
ONE PROOF-OF-PURCHASE

079-KBZ-R

To collect your fabulous FREE GIFT, a cubic zirconia pendant, you must include this original proof-of-purchase for each gift with the properly completed Free Gift Certificate.

079-KBZ-R

Don't miss...

MACKENZIE'S PLEASURE

by *New York Times* bestselling author

LINDA HOWARD

Mackenzie's Mountain. Mackenzie's Mission. In February 1996, bestselling author Linda Howard continues the Mackenzie family saga with *Mackenzie's Pleasure*, IM #691.

Zane Mackenzie was a soldier through and through. He was the best—the only man for the worst of jobs. Then he rescued sweet Barrie Lovejoy from her hellish captivity, and in the desperate hours of the night sealed both their fates. Because danger hadn't ended with Barrie's release. The enemy was still only a heartbeat away—even as Barrie felt the first stirrings of life within her....

Mackenzie's Pleasure—
the book you've been waiting for...
from one of the genre's finest, only in—

LHOW1

You're About to Become a *Privileged Woman*

Reap the rewards of fabulous free gifts and benefits with proofs-of-purchase from Silhouette and Harlequin books

Pages & Privileges™

It's our way of thanking you for buying our books at your favorite retail stores.

PROOF OF PURCHASE
YT-PP103
Offer expires October 31, 1996

Pages & Privileges ™

**Harlequin and Silhouette—
the most privileged readers in the world!**

For more information about Harlequin and Silhouette's PAGES & PRIVILEGES program call the Pages & Privileges Benefits Desk: 1-503-794-2499

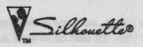

Silhouette®

YT-PP103